Finally, My Forever

Hearts Can Mend

A.P. Spencer

BK
ROYSTON
Publishing

BK Royston Publishing
Jeffersonville, IN
http://www.bkroystonpublishing.com
bkroystonpublishing@gmail.com

Cover Design: Elite Cover Designs
Back Cover Photo: Silent Night Studios

ISBN-13: 978-1-959543-88-6

Printed in the United States of America

Dedication

I dedicate this book to my husband who supports me unconditionally and to my children whom I adore.

Acknowledgements

Thank you, Julia, for listening to me when I told you about the book and the support you have so graciously given to me.

Thank you to my husband and friends who supported me during the process.

Finally, thanks to girlfriends who sit around the table and share their life stories with me.

Table of Contents

Introduction

This books premise is that women never have to settle. Believe you deserve the best and the best will come find you.

This is a work of fiction. All of the characters, organizations, and events portrayed in this novel are either products of the author's imagination or are used fictitiously.

To my husband, who supports me unconditionally.

To my children, whom I adore.

Ann

Part One

"I'll take a beer," Nicole said as she leaned over the bar in the noisy club her friend Trish had brought her to on Friday night.

Trish had said she was becoming a recluse and needed a night out. A Friday night when Nicole would much rather be home watching TV than be out at a bar called Wally's Bar and Grill. Calling this place, a "grill" was a stretch, Nicole thought to herself.

The bartender slid the beer bottle to her.

A deep voice on her left called out over the music, "Nicole... Nicole Berger?"

Nicole turned to see a face from the past and instantly remembered his name.

Brad Reynolds. He had bright blue eyes and was smiling at her. Her heart did a little flip inside her chest.

"Oh, hi, Brad. Yes, it's Nicole, but my last name is now Chapman." Or at least it was. She was considering changing it after the divorce but was concerned about how that would make the kids feel.

Brad looked good, really good, but he always did. He moved a little closer.

"I haven't seen you since high school graduation. You ended up with that guy, Chuck something?" Brad asked as he took a swig of his beer.

"Charles Chapman," Nicole responded. She really didn't want to discuss her ex-husband. Charles would have been furious about that comment. He hated any variation of his name. He always stated that his name was Charles A. Chapman, not Chuck, not Charlie. It was always Charles.

"Hmm," Brad said as he appeared a little baffled. "I don't remember him exactly, but I would know you anywhere."

Nicole knew she was turning bright red. "Me?" she replied.

"How could you remember me?"

Brad leaned in closer and turned on the charm he was always known for back in the high school days, "Because you were the prettiest girl at Wright High School, and you would never have anything to do with me."

Nicole smiled. She was glad she wasn't home watching TV.

High School Days

Nicole walked through the school hallway looking for Charles. He was a senior at the same high school as Nicole and they had been dating for a few months. Nothing serious, Charles said they were too young to be serious, but Nicole was falling fast for him. There was something about him and the way he was always in control that drew her to him. He was so confident whereas Nicole was more indecisive and nervous. Nicole's parents were artists who never lived life by a schedule and were carefree about most everything, including raising their only daughter. Nicole didn't receive that family trait and her parents sometimes told her she needed to chill out more—typical hippy philosophy.

Charles didn't like to chill out. When Charles and Nicole studied together, Charles would often say that they needed to get the best grades, not simply good, but all A's. So, as Nicole's parents looked on and sighed, Nicole pushed herself hard to get all A's in her classes so she would make Charles proud. If that made her a goody-two-shoes, as her dad jokingly called her, then so be it.

In the middle of the hallway was a group of seniors. Nicole cringed inside because she was going to have to walk right by them to get to her next class. These were the "cool" kids who were the gossip of the school. They drank beer and smoked cigarettes and were always in some sort of trouble. Charles didn't approve of their behavior and encouraged Nicole not to listen to the stories about them.

"Hey, Nicky, how are you doing?" a voice beside her asked. Nicole looked sideways. It was Brad Reynolds. Brad was the most popular guy in the senior class. He also had a reputation and many a girl's heart was broken by the notorious Brad.

"Hi, Brad," Nicole said quietly and walked a little faster.

"Hey, wait up," Brad said, moving alongside her. "Where are you going so fast?"

"Class is about to start and I don't want to be late. Goodbye," Nicole walked even faster to lose Brad. She heard the snickers from his group of friends.

Brad called out, "Bye now, Nicky," and turned back to his friends.

Nicole let out her breath and looked down the hallway to see Charles standing by the door of the classroom. He had a look on his face Nicole didn't recognize.

When Nicole got closer, Charles grabbed her arm, a little harder than she thought was necessary.

"What were you doing talking to him?" he asked under his breath.

"I, uh, I wasn't, I-I mean, I didn't t-talk to him," Nicole stammered.

"I saw you talk to him. Don't ever lie to me again, Nicole, or we are through. Do you understand me?" Charles whispered in her ear.

Nicole's eyes filled with sudden tears, "Yes, I understand. I won't talk to him ever again. Are you mad at me Charles?"

Charles' face changed back to the stoic expression he usually wore as he looked down at Nicole.

"No, I am not mad. Just remember, you are my girlfriend and I have high expectations for us."

Nicole was suddenly elated. Charles had never used the term "girlfriend" in their relationship. Her tears turned to joy, and she wiped her cheeks and followed Charles into their class.

Brad heard the bell ring for class but didn't move from where he stood as he tried to understand what he had just witnessed between Nicole and Charles at the end of the hall. 'What was she doing with a guy like him?' Brad shrugged and jogged to class, where a quick smile to the female teacher made his tardy excuse easy to accept.

Years later, Nicole would remember that event and wonder why she ever let Charles take control of her life.

Charles

Nicole married Charles after college. There had never been anyone else for her but Charles. The proposal was intimate and beautiful. He wrote a poem to her and proposed on bended knee. Of course, Nicole said yes immediately. Her parents were a little skeptical, but nothing could stand in the way of Charles when he wanted something. He had very strong ideas about her wedding dress, the church and the vows. It was like he was the bridezilla of the wedding instead of Nicole. He wanted the dress to be very modest, so Nicole found a dress with truly little cleavage, and she let Charles handle the vows. While she was trying on the dress, her mother made a comment that she should just cut a hole in a blanket and wear that for her wedding dress, that would be just as attractive as the dress she picked out for the wedding.

Nicole didn't respond; she loved the way she looked in her dress. Charles also told her before the wedding that he felt that the word "obey" should be part of her vows to him and he would use the words "respect and cherish" in his vows to her. Nicole was so in love with Charles and excited to be married that she would have promised him anything.

The wedding was small and perfect in Nicole's eyes. Charles looked so handsome standing at the end of the aisle on the alter. His father was his best man. Charles had told her he didn't have any friends that he felt were right for such an important day, so he had his father stand with him. Later, Nicole would think it odd that he had no friends at the wedding.

What kind of man doesn't have any friends to stand up for him?

She pledged to love and obey Charles and he said he would love and protect her until death do them part. There was a small gathering at a local reception hall, and after cutting the cake, Charles and Nicole were both careful to feed each other a small piece. Charles had said before the wedding there was to be no nonsense with the cake, which was for people who don't respect the sanctity of marriage. After a few awkward dances with the family, Charles and Nicole were off to the hotel for their wedding night.

There had been some heavy make-out sessions before the wedding, but Nicole didn't have any experience with sex and didn't really know what to expect. Her mother had tried to explain the intimacy between a husband and wife, but Nicole was still painfully shy as she came out of the hotel bathroom in her white nightgown. Charles was clearly aroused by her and was gentle with his lovemaking. Nicole was slightly surprised how quickly the interaction ended. Charles held her in his arms, and they fell asleep.

At the time, Nicole didn't know any better about the complexity of married life. She thought all husbands were supposed to be the head of the home and what they said and what they wanted went without question. Her parents had a very casual marriage, one Nicole didn't quite understand. She liked the structure that Charles brought to their relationship and marriage. After a quick honeymoon to Florida, Charles sat Nicole down one afternoon in their apartment. She was being given a weekly allowance for expenses and Charles requested that if she wanted to go somewhere without him, she needed to let him know where she was going. Nicole didn't care at the time about his "rules" since she was so in love with Charles, and she followed whatever he said.

They eventually bought a house in a nice little cul-de-sac and Nicole started work at a local bank while Charles worked at the Chapman Investment Firm which had been started by his father. "That's where I get my money sense," Charles would say as he handed Nicole her weekly allowance in a white envelope.

"Remember," he would say, "when that's gone, the well is dry until next week."

Wally's Bar and Grill

Brad

Brad and Nicole talked until the wee hours of the morning. Trish had left earlier when Brad said he would make sure Nicole got home safely. Nicole felt odd being left alone in a bar with Brad, but she also felt more alive like she had felt in a long time. She had never sat in a bar with Charles, talking and laughing, until 2:00 am.

"I will tell you one thing, Nic," Brad said. "I am never getting married again."

"Me, either!" Nicole replied, laughing with Brad. It felt good to laugh; she took a moment and tried to remember when the last time was that she had laughed, and her mind went blank.

"Hey, where are you, Nic?" Brad asked. "Don't go back down memory lane, it's not a fun trip."

It turns out that Brad had gone through a divorce also and had two girls from the marriage. He said he got along okay with his ex, unlike Nicole and her relationship with Charles.

"We communicate for the kids, but that's all," Nicole explained. "I can't let him in my life again to let him treat me the way he did when we were married."

"Did he hurt you?" Brad asked as he sat up a little straighter in his chair.

"Not physically," Nicole replied. "But he messed with my head so much that I couldn't see the truth in our relationship."

"What a jerk," Brad replied. "I'm glad you're not with him anymore."

With a big smile, Nicole tapped her beer to Brad's and laughed, "Me too, Brad. Me too."

Charles

Married life with Charles was consistent and steady, and if Nicole admitted it, frankly, sometimes boring. Charles liked things to be calm and quiet. But most of all, he did not like his decisions questioned. Nicole didn't even think of questioning him.

One evening, Nicole and Charles were out talking to some of their neighbors when another fellow neighbor made a comment about their lawn and how Charles needed to mow his yard. Charles laughed and joked with everyone that he was going to let the grass grow knee high. Even Nicole laughed at the absurd comment.

When they went inside the house for dinner, Charles was furious. "How dare that SOB tell me how to take care of my yard!" he yelled.

He turned to Nicole and shouted at her, "And you laughed right along with him. Do you know how humiliating that was for me?"

Nicole was speechless that such a small comment could send Charles into a rage.

"Charles," Nicole started, "I'm sorry, I didn't mean to embarrass you." Nicole knew by now the easiest way to calm Charles down was to apologize and take the blame. "I was wrong to laugh, and by the way, he doesn't know what he is talking about. Our yard is much better looking than his."

Charles paused and then turned around to Nicole. He had a strange look in his eyes.

"You are right, Nicole. Our yard is better." He leaned in close to Nicole, "But you are never to talk to him or his wife ever again. Do you understand me?"

"Yes, of course," Nicole replied. "I will never talk to them again."

A few days later, the same neighbors' little dog disappeared and was never found. That was the first time that Nicole felt unsettled and wondered if Charles had had anything to do with the dog's disappearance.

Because Charles was so limited with his emotions and money, Nicole was shocked one night at dinner when he suggested they start a family. Nicole had always wanted a family and they had discussed it, but she never got the feeling that Charles wanted children. Charles would later tell everyone it was his idea to start a family and he had to convince Nicole of the idea.

Nicole became pregnant quickly and Charles played the part of a doting husband. He pampered Nicole and helped with dinner and chores around the house, chores that he had always said were her responsibility. He went to the doctor's appointment with her, and at the ultrasound appointment, he had tears in his eyes as they watched their baby move.

"Do you want to know the sex of the baby?" the ultrasound technician asked.

"Yes, we want to know," Charles answered. Nicole knew he would want to know the sex of the baby because Charles hated surprises.

The technician glanced at Nicole, and she nodded her head.

"You are having a boy," she replied. Charles stood up and clapped his hands together.

"Yes, I knew I would make a son." Charles was ecstatic.

Well, it takes two to tango," the technician replied as she was wiping off Nicole's stomach. Nicole froze. Charles didn't like to be reprimanded.

Charles looked at the technician and said very clearly, "How do I know the baby is mine? Is there a test or something to make sure it's my child?"

Nicole sat up quickly, "Charles, of course, it's your child. Please!"

The technician looked back and forth between Nicole and Charles. "I am sorry if I implied anything. I spoke out of turn."

Charles had a smug look on his face. He loved to win a fight and make other people apologize for no reason. As Nicole and Charles were leaving the doctor's office, he leaned in and whispered into Nicole's ear, "That kid better look like me or there is going to be a problem." Nicole kept quiet. It was just easier not to say anything when he was in this kind of mood.

Brad

The ride home to Nicole's condo was quiet. Nicole had not been in a car with another man except one since Charles. She told Brad she and the kids had been living with her mom until she could get back on her feet financially and she now had her own place. Pulling up in front of the condo, Nicole was a nervous wreck.

Brad turned to her and looked at her for a minute, then said, "Nic, can I get your cell number? Do you want to go out sometime?"

Nicole couldn't speak. She just stared at Brad.

"Okay, well, you don't have to give me your number," Brad laughed.

"No, no, here, I will write it down for you," Nicole said as she fumbled in her purse for a pen and a piece of paper.

After she gave Brad her number and he offered to walk her to the door, which she declined, she let herself into the house and leaned back against the door. She had just given her number to the bad guy from high school, and she couldn't be more excited. Nicole had her head in the clouds thinking Brad would be calling her soon.

Her mom, Claire, invited her over for breakfast the next day and made the comment, "Someone looks like they were out late last night," as she poured Nicole and herself a cup of coffee.

"Do you want to talk about it?" she coyly asked.

Nicole hesitated. She usually told her mom everything. She had been Nicole's rock when her marriage ended and she had nowhere to live, but for some reason, Nicole wanted to keep Brad and their meeting to herself.

"I just saw some people from high school last night and it was fun to catch up," Nicole responded sipping her coffee.

"Mm hm," said her mother as she headed out of the kitchen. "You hated high school."

Charles

"Push, one, two, three," the nurse counted as Nicole pushed with all her strength to bring their son into the world.

"You are doing great, Nicole, keep pushing!" Charles urged her on. He loved having the opportunity to tell her what to do when she wished he would just be quiet. With another push, Charles Bennett Chapman III came into the world. Nicole wanted to call their son Andrew after her father, but Charles wouldn't hear of it. "We will honor my father by naming him after the men in my family."

Nicole didn't have the energy to argue with her husband. It had been a long pregnancy and labor, and immediately she and Charles were in love with their tiny son.

When the new family got home from the hospital, everything was perfect. Charles helped her with feedings and diaper duty. There was no mention of little Charles not being his child. The baby had his same hazel brown eyes and blond hair. He was a beautiful baby and easy to take care of.

Nicole's mother visited frequently to see her new grandson and, one afternoon, asked Nicole a question. "How in the world did you agree to the name Charles III? What an old-fashioned name for such a small child. Are you going to put Charles III on his backpack?"

Nicole quietly shushed her. "Mom, it's the name we agreed upon. Please stop," as she rocked the baby.

Later that evening, Charles was quiet at dinner.

"Are you okay, honey?" Nicole asked.

"I think it would be better if your mother does not come back over for a while," he said, looking down at his untouched plate of food. "I don't think she respects our wishes, and I would prefer her not to be in my own house with my child." With that, he got up and left the table.

Nicole closed her eyes; he must have overheard her mother earlier that day. Her mother was her only friend allowed in the house, and now she was going to lose her too. Nicole put her head in her hands and silently sobbed.

Eventually, Nicole's mother was allowed back over, but Nicole's social circle remained tightly controlled by Charles. He was obsessed with little Charles and spent all his spare time holding him and rocking him to sleep. Nicole's maternity leave was two weeks from ending, and after putting the baby to bed, she came back into the living room and sat beside Charles on the sofa.

"I can't believe I have to go back to work in two weeks," Nicole began. "I am going to miss Little Charles so much. Did you have a chance to check out the day care I have reserved for him to go to?"

"I have it all taken care of," Charles replied as he watched TV. "My mother will take care of him for us."

"Your mom?" Nicole looked at Charles. "Your mom is pretty active with her golf and Bridge club.

Are you sure she wants to watch Little Charles full time?"

"Are you saying she isn't a good grandmother?" Charles replied, looking at Nicole. "She raised me, and I turned out pretty good if you ask me." He shook his head.

"Charles, darling," Nicole was trying to diffuse the situation before it got heated. "Of course, she is a good mother and grandmother, I just didn't know she had any interest in watching the baby full time."

"My mother and I talked, and we feel that's what's best for Little Charles. End of discussion."

Nicole laid her head on Charles' shoulder and closed her eyes. *'There was never any discussion,'* she thought to herself.

As it turned out, Charles's mother didn't last one week watching her grandson. Feeding a baby breast milk and changing dirty diapers was not her cup of tea, and she missed a Bridge game. She also pitched a fit about calling the baby 'Little Charles.'

"Who thought of that nickname?" she asked. "It's ridiculous."

Charles and his father looked at each other. Nicole just looked down at her hands.

"If I have to call this baby 'Little Charles' then I am going to start calling you 'Big Charles,' she said staring at Charles. Turning to her husband, she continued, "And that makes you Old Charles!"

Nicole had to look out the window in order not to laugh. Charles and his father looked at each other, aghast.

"Nicole, what's his middle name again?" she asked.

Nicole carefully covered her shock. What grandmother forgets her first grandchild's middle name?

"His middle name is Bennett," Nicole responded.

"There you go!" she exclaimed. "We can call him Ben." She picked up the baby from the bassinet and held him in her arms. "Hello there, sweet baby Ben. It's your Grand. Not Grandmother, I'm your Grand."

So, the issue of Ben's name and Charles' mother's nickname was settled, and Big and Old Charles didn't say a peep.

Ben did well at his daycare and Nicole reveled in the camaraderie of the other moms at the daycare. When she picked up Ben after work, she looked forward to chatting with the other moms about mundane things like formula or when they were starting solid foods. It was an opportunity for her to grow as a mother, and Nicole loved it. Charles didn't like taking the baby to daycare because he had an aversion to germs and when he saw all the drooling babies, he quickly decided it was Nicole's responsibility to drop off Ben and pick him up. Nicole made the most of every moment alone with her son. She sang to him on the way to daycare and played silly songs on the radio. It was her time with her son that she had all to herself because as soon as she got home, she had to get dinner started and then bathe Ben and put him to bed.

Working full-time and having a small baby was exhausting and Nicole was trying her best to keep up a brave face, but she needed help. Most of the baby's costs fell on her, such as the diapers and daycare, and her salary at work barely covered it all. She still received her "allowance" from Charles and decided it was time to ask for more money.

One night, after dinner when Nicole had put the baby to bed, she approached Charles while he was watching TV.

"Sweetie," Nicole began. "I really need your advice." Nicole had been thinking of a way to bring up the subject.

"What's the matter, dear?" Charles looked away from the TV at her.

"I am having a hard time making ends meet and you are so good with money, I know you can help me," Nicole started. Nicole knew Charles loved to feel needed and in control, so she appealed to that part of his personality.

"Hmm," Charles replied. "Let's go crunch some numbers."

The last thing Nicole wanted to do was sit at the kitchen table and "crunch numbers" with Charles, but if that would get her more money, then she would do anything. About an hour later, Charles sat back and scratched his head. Nicole produced all the baby's bills, from daycare to his formula, and then added in the grocery bill for the family. For every pushback from Charles, she had a receipt of a cost she covered. Her final card was something she was holding in her back pocket.

"I don't know why I even work. It would be cheaper if I stayed home and raised Ben," Nicole began.

"Wait one minute! You cover all the benefits, and I can't afford to take that on right now. I am putting a lot of money away for us and the kids and we need your salary," Charles exclaimed. He looked down at the tabletop again, now covered with receipts, and sighed. "I am going to give you more money for your allowance. You must work; I don't see how we can live on one salary. I am glad you asked for my help," Charles said, reaching across the table for Nicole's hand. "That's why I manage the money for the family."

Nicole smiled brightly at Charles. "Yes, you are so smart, Charles. I am so glad we have you." Nicole meant what she said, but she also felt like she had won a major battle and that felt wonderful.

Brad

Nicole looked down at her cell phone and put it face down on her desktop.

"What's up with you today?" Trish asked. "You're not acting like yourself."

"He hasn't called," Nicole replied.

"Did he say he would?" Trish asked.

"Yes, I told you everything he said to me in the car. He asked for my number," Nicole responded.

"Maybe he lost your number, or maybe he's just being a guy and making you wait. You know, guys are weird about stuff like that," Trish replied trying to cheer Nicole up.

"Hey!" Trish said. "Why don't you call him?"

Nicole looked shocked. "Girls don't call guys. That's not appropriate." She turned back to her computer and started typing furiously.

Trish turned back to her work and said over her shoulder, "Welcome to the 21st century. Girls call guys all the time. But don't worry. I am sure he will show up on a mounted steed to whisk you away on a date. Just like in the movies you like to watch."

Later that night after the kids were in bed, Nicole stared down at her phone again. No new calls. She knew from the night at the bar where Brad worked. 'Should I call him tomorrow?' she asked herself. Nicole's thoughts were all over the place. She thought they had really made a connection the night they met.

'Oh, my word,' Nicole thought, 'you drank some beers with a guy from high school who was, and is, way out of your league and you are using a word like "connection?" You sound like one of those dating shows that Trish watches all the time.' Disgusted with herself and feeling a little foolish, she put the phone on her bedside table and turned over to go to sleep.

Wednesday was a mess. The kids didn't get out of practice until late, and it was raining cats and dogs, traffic was terrible, so by the time they all got home, Nicole was frustrated to say the least. When they piled in the door, there was no plan for dinner, and everyone was hungry.

Great, thought Nicole, *what can I microwave for a decent meal?* as she rummaged through the freezer.

Her cell phone vibrated in her pocket, and she reached for it, answering with a gruff, "Hello?"

"Nicole, hey, it's Brad. Did I call at a bad time?"

Nicole froze. Her mind frantically tried to think of something to say.

"Nicole?" Brad asked.

"Oh, hey, Brad. Sorry, I didn't recognize the number," she replied.

"No problem," Brad said. "It's good to hear your voice. I wanted to call sooner but I was out of town the beginning of this week and the kids had games last night. When I have a chance to spend time with them, I take it," Brad explained.

Nicole kicked off her shoes and sat down. Dinner could wait a few more minutes.

"I'm glad you got to spend time with your children. It seems like they grow up so fast." *Duh! Such a typical thing to say,* thought Nicole.

"How was work today?" Brad asked.

Nicole paused. She couldn't ever remember Charles asking how her day was, so Brad's question caught her off guard.

"It was good, for a Wednesday. Except traffic tonight was terrible," Nicole replied.

They both chatted for a few more minutes about the weather and other trivial things.

"Nicole, would you like to grab some dinner this weekend?" he asked.

Nicoles mind raced ahead to the weekend. The kids would be with Charles, and the only thing she had going on was another weekend in bed watching old movies.

"Nicole, don't make a guy wait so long for an answer. It takes a hit to my self-confidence," Brad joked.

She laughed and replied, "Brad, you are the most confident person I know. And, yes, I am free this weekend."

"Great! I'll pick you up about 6:00 Saturday night, at your house," Brad said.

"That sounds good. See you then, Brad," Nicole replied. As she hung up from the call, she smiled and twirled around in the kitchen. She had a date Saturday night for the first time in a very long

time.

Charles

By all outside accounts, anyone would think that the Chapmans were a perfect suburban family. Charles and Nicole were young and good looking. Ben was so cute as he peddled his tricycle around the cul-de -sac. They were cordial to the neighbors, but no one had ever been inside their house, and that's the way Charles wanted it. He said to Nicole once that he had so much interaction with other people at work every day that he enjoyed the quiet at home. Nicole didn't mind the quiet. Charles would play on his phone or work on his computer and Nicole would go watch TV by herself when Ben went to bed.

One weekend, Charles was in a great mood and was back to his old charming self. He grilled steaks outside, opened a bottle of wine and even helped clean up the kitchen. Nicole put Ben down to bed a little early to get back to spending time with Charles. As Charles and Nicole finished off the bottle of wine and watched the sun set, Nicole felt warm and content, and she liked this feeling. Charles reached out for her hand, and they sat hand in hand until the sun went down. Nicole didn't know if it was the wine or the change in his mood, but when they made love that night, it felt as if they really connected to each other. Nicole fell asleep and slept soundly throughout the night.

Life had its routine with Nicole taking Ben to preschool and then going to work. Charles said the firm he worked at with his father was doing very well, and Nicole had no reason to doubt him. He said they had money in the bank and were growing a large savings account, mostly due to the fact they rarely went out and were very frugal with their money, especially Charles. Nicole's mom would offer to watch Ben so they could have a date night, but Charles would always reply, "I have everything right here to make it a date night," so they didn't go out on dates.

With Nicole still on an allowance, she brought her lunch to work most days, but one day decided to go out to eat at a local Mexican restaurant with the girls from work. Nicole had a great time and got to know one of the new girls named Trish. Trish was everything Nicole was not. She was loud, funny and flirted with any man who crossed her path. Nicole was envious of Trish and her outlook on life, but then remembered that Trish was single, and she had a husband and a son, whom she both adored.

One day, Nicole wasn't feeling well, and her boss let her go home early. She asked her mom to pick up Ben at preschool and bring him home as she didn't want to spread anything if she was sick. Nicole lay down on the bed and fell into a deep sleep, only to be awakened when Ben jumped on the bed and started telling her about his school day. Nicole's mom came over and put her hand on Nicole's forehead and commented, "You don't feel warm."

Nicole replied, " I am just so tired lately. I can barely keep my eyes open."

Nicole and her mother looked at each other.

"I'll run down to the drug store and be right back," her mom said.

The next morning, Nicole got up early and went to the bathroom. Two minutes later, she had the results. She sat on the edge of the tub with her head in her hand.

She was pregnant.

Charles was ecstatic. Unlike her previous pregnancy, when he had made comments about the paternity, there were no comments this time around. When Grace Ann was born eight months later, Charles wept when he held her.

He looked at Nicole and said, "Thank you for my beautiful princess."

Nicole smiled at the scene of Charles holding Grace; he was obviously besotted with his infant daughter. *Things are going to be perfect now,* Nicole thought. *We have two beautiful children. What else could we wish for?*

Brad

Nicole told Trish she was going out on a date with Brad when they were at lunch the next day, and Trish was about as excited as Nicole.

"What are you going to wear?" she asked. "How are you going to wear your hair? Please tell me you are going to ditch the ponytail look for the date," she added.

Nicole absent-mindedly reached back and touched her hair. She had worn her hair pulled back for all her marriage, that's how Charles had liked It. He said her face was too beautiful to hide behind hair, but now she wondered if that had really been the truth.

"Are you going to do something about those nails?" Trish continued. "Ugh, I thought you said you stopped chewing your nails," she said, pulling Nicole's hands close to inspect her nail beds. "I am calling my girl right now and getting you in for a manicure," Trish exclaimed.

"Okay," Nicole reluctantly agreed. It was an expense she really couldn't afford but her nails did look terrible.

"One last thing," Trish whispered as she slid her chair close to Nicole's and glanced down at her lap. "Do you need a bikini wax?" She laughed out loud as only Trish could do.

"No, thank you! You are terrible!" Nicole laughed. That was the reason she loved Trish. She always said something crazy to make Nicole laugh and blush.

Ben and Grace were not as thrilled as Trish that she was going out on a date. The divorce had been very difficult for them, and they were both still very supportive of their father, even though they didn't live with him full time.

"I am glad we will be going over to Dad's on Saturday," Ben mentioned at dinner. "I think he's lonely."

Nicole didn't respond. She knew firsthand how lonely felt, but she didn't want to make this into a competition to see which parent was the loneliest.

"I'll be glad to drop you off at your dad's Saturday. Just text him and make sure he will be home," Nicole replied as she started gathering up the dinner dishes.

Both kids helped clear the table then disappeared to their rooms. Sometimes, in the quiet moments of the evening, Nicole wondered if she should have tried harder to make her marriage work. But the betrayal was just too deep.

Charles

Nothing was too good for Charles' children. Both Ben and Grace had the best of everything. Charles insisted they go to the best private schools—no public schools for his children, even though Nicole had heard good things about the local schools. If either of the children wanted to play a sport, they were decked out in the newest garb. Charles only insisted on one thing: whatever they started; they couldn't quit because they didn't like it.

One soccer season, Nicole and Charles sat and watched Ben attempt to play soccer even though it was apparent to everyone but his father that he wasn't very good at the sport. Still, Charles made it to every game to cheer his son on from the sidelines.

Charles and Nicole were at every dance recital for Grace, and at the end of her performance, he would stand and cheer for her. Nicole thought it was a bit of overkill, but Grace enjoyed her father's attention.

One weekend afternoon while they were all over at Charles parents' house, Nicole and his mom, Peggy, were in the kitchen when Nicole brought up how supportive Charles was of the children's extracurricular activities.

"Good! I am so glad," Peggy replied. "Charles' father never went to any of his games, too busy at work. I remember seeing Charles looking up in the stands, hoping to see his dad in a seat, but it never happened. I am glad Charles is different."

"Me too," Nicole said. "Me too."

Nicole was determined to have a change of heart regarding how Charles supported their children. As far as she could see at the children's events, it was mostly moms, not a lot of dads. She was suddenly very proud of her husband.

Nicole walked up behind Charles as he stood outside watching Ben practice his soccer moves. She wrapped her arms around him from behind and laid her head on his back.

"Whoa!" Charles laughed. "What is this about?"

"I just think you are awesome and wanted to thank you for all you do for me and the kids. You are a really good father," Nicole whispered.

Charles looked back at Nicole for a minute. "Thank you, babe. That means a lot to me."

He turned back to Ben, "Keep practicing, son. Next year, you will be on the starting team. Go get 'em!"

"Go, Ben! You got this!" Nicole cheered.

Their son looked up at both of his parents cheering him on and kicked the soccer ball directly in the goal.

So, time began to fly by for Nicole. As it turned out, Ben made the soccer team at his school and started the games instead of sitting on the bench. His father credited it to his coaching, but it was really the fact that Ben himself wouldn't give up until he was very good at the sport. Grace was still dancing, but as a young girl, she was more interested in makeup and hair than dance practice, but she still went because she didn't want to disappoint her father.

"Remember," Charles would begin, "we are not the quitting type of family."

Brad

It was 6:05 and no Brad.

Nicole had a thought, 'What if he stands me up?' She began pacing the room. 'Why isn't he here yet?'

At 6:10, the doorbell rang. Nicole opened the door and there was Brad, with a smile on his face and flowers in his hands.

"I'm sorry I am late, but I didn't want to arrive empty-handed for our first date," he said as he offered Nicole the flowers, "and I had no idea the grocery store would be so packed."

"Come in," Nicole said, standing back so he could come into the condo. "I'll put the flowers in water before we leave." She started towards the kitchen.

"Hey, Nicole?" Brad asked. "Um, you look really good and nice and stuff, but I thought we were going out for a casual dinner?"

Nicole looked down at her blouse and skirt and then took in Brad's shirt and jeans.

"Too much?" Nicole asked.

"Well, maybe for dinner tonight, unless you want to go somewhere fancy. I thought we could go somewhere where we can talk and not feel rushed," Brad responded.

"That sounds perfect!" Nicole said as she put the flowers in a vase. "Let me run upstairs and change."

Five minutes later, Nicole came down the stairs in jeans and a black leather jacket. "Is this better?" she asked Brad.

Brad looked at her up and down from head to toe. "Much!" he said. "Let's go get some dinner."

An hour later, Nicole popped the last French fry in her mouth and exclaimed, "Wow, that was great!"

Brad stared at her and at her empty plate.

"Did I do something wrong?" Nicole asked, the insecurities of her past creeping back in.

"No, not at all," Brad replied. "I like a girl who loves a burger and fries and doesn't eat a salad at every meal."

The date was fun. Brad and Nicole enjoyed the food and each other's company. Brad opened up about his time after high school. He went to college and, after the first semester, decided that college wasn't for him.

"I didn't flunk out; in fact, I had great grades which made my decision to come back home hard on my parents, but I didn't want to go down the frat boy route. So, I moved back home. I got a job with a friend of my dad's and loved it. I went back to community college to learn more about business development and now I pretty much run the business."

Nicole was impressed. She hadn't kept up with anyone from high school and just assumed he had gone off to party at college with all his high school buddies.

Brad had two girls with his ex-wife with whom he was still on good terms. He told Nicole he was too young when they got married but he loved his girls with all of his heart. The way Brad spoke to Nicole about the past few years made it a little uncomfortable for her to go into detail about why she and Charles had split up. She chalked it up to having it being held down so long and their odd marriage. Brad had shown her more emotion in the last hour than Charles had shown her in the last few years of their marriage.

"Hello over there? Are you still with me?" Brad asked as he reached out to touch Nicole's hand.

Nicole jumped but then grabbed Brad's hand back as he started to withdraw it across the table.

"Yes, I am here," Nicole answered. "It's just my story is a little harder to tell. I know the first night we met, I told you some things about my marriage, but it has a darker side that is hard for me to discuss," She looked at Brad.

"Did the SOB lay a hand on you?" Brad asked quickly. He looked like he would get up from the table, go find Charles and punch his lights out.

"No, Brad, he never hit me. It was something that took me a long time to realize what he was doing to us. It was all about ownership and power with Charles. And then one day, I decided to take my power back."

Charles

Nicole was back to a full-time job now that the children were older and was delighted to see her old friend Trish was still at the same company and had an office just down the hall from her. They hugged each other and went to grab a cup of coffee. Trish said, "I can't believe it's been so long! The last time we talked was when you found out you were pregnant with Grace."

"I can't believe how times flies, " Nicole said. "Tell me, what's going on with you?"

It turns out Trish had found the man of her dreams and they had run off to Vegas to get married—so typical Trish—and they were thinking about starting a family.

"I think being a mother is the best thing I ever did," Nicole replied as she looked at the pictures of her children on her desk. "I would do anything for them".

"What about the hubs?" Trish asked. "I don't see a picture of Chucky on your desk."

"Everything is fine," Nicole replied quickly. "We are both busy with the kids; it's hard to find time to be alone together." The truth was Nicole could feel the distance growing between them and was concerned about their marriage.

"Well, you two have been together a long time. Maybe you need to spice things up?" And with that, Trish began to describe a negligee she received for her honeymoon and the results it had on her husband.

"Trish!" Nicole laughed. "I am so glad I am back."

Truth be told, things were busy at home but not unmanageable. Nicole couldn't remember when she started to feel like she was being controlled by Charles, but things were changing for her. There was no change in the amount of her "weekly allowance" from him, so she started to put money back from her check at work to spend on herself. What was puzzling was that Charles had no spending limits when it came to the children, but he seemed to take some pleasure in handing her the envelope with her weekly allowance on Monday mornings.

Lately, he'd started with a wise-crack comment as he reached in to kiss her goodbye and hand her the envelope.

He would whisper, "Don't spend it all in one place, that's all you have for the week."

Since this had been going on through their whole marriage, Nicole just assumed that all couples had a budget, and the husband controlled the finances. She really didn't have any close friends outside of work, so she decided to bring up the topic with Trish one day at lunch.

"I see you are still packing your lunch," Trish commented, sliding in the booth across from Nicole in the lunchroom.

"Yes, I am all about saving money," Nicole replied, unpacking her salad.

"Ugh, I wish Matt would learn that trick. He loves to go out and spend money and I must remind him that we need to be saving up for a house. Thank

goodness, I can manage our bank accounts online,"
Trish responded.

"Don't you have a checkbook?" Nicole asked.
Charles kept the checkbook in the desk where the
bills were kept. Nicole didn't think she had ever
opened the desk to look at their account
information.

"That's old school!" Trish said. "You can do
everything online now with your bank."

Seeing Nicole's confused expression, Trish
asked, "Don't you have an online bank account?"

"No," Nicole said, looking down at her salad.
"Charles takes care of all of that."

"What? What if something happened and you
had to get some cash? You have a debit card, don't
you?" Trish asked, looking over the table at Nicole.

"No. I get an allowance each week from Charles, and he manages all of the money and bills," Nicole said.

Trish sat across from Nicole with a look of shock on her face. "You get an allowance? You are his wife, not a five-year-old who gets a dollar for taking out the trash. Are you being serious with me right now?" Trish demanded.

Nicole looked at her friend with a sad expression. "Yes, I am serious, and I am starting to think I am being taken advantage of," Nicole replied.

Trish reached across the table and whispered to Nicole, "Tell me everything."

Nicole told her everything, starting with the fact that Charles was the only man she had ever kissed or had sex with. She told her about his control over her life, limiting her interaction with the neighbors, and how Charles gave her a weekly allowance and she had no idea how much money they had in the bank. She told her that after all these years with Charles, she was beginning to feel like something wasn't right between them, but she couldn't pinpoint what it was.

After Nicole finished her story, Trish leaned back and sighed. "Wow," was all she could say.

Then Trish asked, "Do you think he is having an affair?"

Brad

It tickled.

Nicole didn't know how else to describe the first kiss with Brad after their date. He walked her to her front door, put his hand under her chin and gave her a slow kiss. His beard tickled her face. She had never kissed another man other than her ex-husband, and she felt this kiss all the way to her toes.

Brad looked at her and whispered, "I had a really good time tonight. Can I see you again?"

"Yes," Nicole whispered back.

Brad walked to his car, but before he got in, he turned around and waved at Nicole.

Damn, thought Nicole, *he still has it,* and let herself into the condo.

Charles

By the end of the day, Nicole had a login to the bank where she and Charles had an account and had ordered a debit card, to be delivered to Trish's home address of course.

Trish also helped her set up a "secret" account at another bank and had a small amount of her check directly deposited into that account. Trish looked at her and patted her hand, "It's called 'just in case' money."

After all the activity, Nicole felt a little better, but the question about Charles having an affair bothered her. Initially, Nicole thought, *No way*, but did she really know that for certain? They both spent every spare minute away from work together with the kids and were still active in the bedroom a couple times a month.

"That doesn't matter," Trish said when Nicole explained her situation. "Men can manipulate any situation if they want something bad enough."

Nicole made an excuse to leave the office at lunchtime the next day and stopped by Charles' office. As she pulled into parking lot, she saw Charles walking to his car with a woman. He opened the passenger side car door for her and then went to his side and got in, and they drove away. Nicole felt sick to her stomach. Why would her husband be going at lunch with another woman? Everything in her wanted to follow his car and find out where they were going together, but then another thought came into her mind. She pulled out of the parking lot and headed back to work.

Later that evening, as she was clearing off the dinner dishes and the kids were in their room doing homework, Nicole said, "I stopped by your office today to see if you could go to lunch, but I must have just missed you." As she turned to see Charles' face, she thought she saw a brief look of panic, but he quickly covered up his expression.

"What?" Charles began, "You have never stopped by my office for lunch. Why start today?" He didn't look very pleased with her dropping by his office.

"Well," Nicole explained, "with this new role at work, I am out of the office more and I thought it would be nice to surprise my handsome husband at work and ask him to take me out to lunch." Nicole wrapped her arms around Charles' shoulders and gave him a kiss.

Charles patted her hands and replied, "You know I don't like surprises, Nicole."

"Yes, I know," Nicole replied. "But it will be fun to pop in and go to lunch together sometime. Don't you think?" she asked as she moved across the room.

"Why don't you text me before you come to the office?" Charles replied. "That way, I can make sure I am free for lunch. I have customers whom I need to meet with and sometimes lunch is a good meeting time for them," he offered.

"Maybe," Nicole said quietly as she left the kitchen. She felt good. She had the upper hand, for now.

Brad

Nicoles second date with Brad was a basketball game and Nicole quickly realized he really got into the game.

"Are you kidding me, ref? Really? Do you want to borrow my glasses so you can see the game?" Brad yelled, then sat down next to Nicole and asked, "Can you believe that call?"

"Do you always do that?" Nicole asked, laughing. "I have never seen this side of you."

"It's my therapy," Brad responded. "I get all my pent-up frustration out at sporting events."

"Okay," Nicole responded. "I'm just glad I am not out there on the court."

Brad turned to look at her and put his hand on her thigh. " I am too. I want you right here by me."

Nicole smiled and was about to respond when Brad yelled, "Come on! That was a terrible call, ref."

Nicole sipped her beer; she was having a great time.

Dates with Brad became more frequent, but they still hadn't introduced their children to each other or even discussed the possibility. Nicole assumed they were only dating each other, but she really didn't know that for a fact. Trish brought it up one day at work.

"So, are you and Brad exclusively dating each other?" she asked at lunch.

Nicole didn't know how to respond. "I guess."

"What do you mean, you guess? It's a yes or no question!" Trish exclaimed. "You need to ask him if he's seeing anyone else. Tonight."

"I don't know," Nicole said. "I don't want to know if he's dating anyone else right now. What we have is pretty good." She didn't want to come across as insecure, even if she was.

She was meeting Brad for an early dinner after work before heading home to the kids. She was already in the booth when he walked into the restaurant. He looked around, and when he spotted Nicole, he broke into a big smile and headed right to her. Nicole's heart always did a little flip when she saw Brad and this time was no different.

"Hey, babe," Brad said as he leaned in for a kiss. "So good to see my girl." He slid in the booth across from Nicole. As always, the conversation was so easy with Brad. They talked about their day and only took a break when their food arrived. After they finished the meal, Brad reached over and took Nicole's hand. Nicole smiled and looked down at her lap.

Trish's voice kept repeating in her head. 'Ask him, Nicole. Ask him,' Trish's voice in her head repeated.

"Nic," Brad started. "I know we haven't been together long, but I can tell something is up with you. What's going on babe?"

Nicole took a deep breath and asked the question. "Are you dating anyone else besides me, Brad?"

"What?" Brad asked as he was laughing. "Where did that come from?"

Nicole felt her cheeks turning red and she turned and looked away.

"Hey, hey, babe. It's okay. I don't want to upset you. Your question just took me by surprise, that's all." Brad grabbed both of her hands. "Nic, look at me," Brad requested.

Nicole looked across the table at him.

Okay," he started, looking down at their intertwined hands. "I am not dating anyone else, and I don't want to. How about you? Do you want to date someone else? Is that what you want to do?" Brad asked.

Nicole's mouth fell open. "What? No, no, no," she replied. "I just didn't know."

"Didn't know what? That I am nuts about you and I don't want to date anyone else. But I have dated after my divorce, and you haven't. Do you want some time off to date other guys? I can understand if you do," Brad was serious.

"Brad," Nicole began, "I know you are only the second guy I have ever dated, but I don't want to date anyone else. I really like what we have together, and I don't need to date anyone else to confirm my feelings for you."

Brad smiled and squeezed her hands. " So, we are only seeing each other and that's good?"

"Yes!" Nicole replied. "And I am probably a little nuts about you too, Brad," she teased.

"Probably! Really? Guess I am going to have to up my game." Brad signaled for the check.

They made out in her car like a couple of teenagers until a woman in the next car yelled, "Get a room!"

Brad looked at Nicole, smiled and said, "Now,

that's a great idea."

Charles

Nicole leaned over the front counter and said to the pretty brunette receptionist, "Is Charles in? I am his wife and I wanted to pop in and say hello to him." Nicole knew Charles was at work, she saw his car in the parking lot when she pulled into his office. The receptionist, who Nicole was pretty sure was the same woman who got into Charles' car with him a few weeks earlier, looked like she had seen a ghost.

"Yes, he's in, Mrs. Chapman. Let me call his office." She picked up the phone and announced to Charles that Nicole was in the lobby.

Charles quickly appeared around the corner. He gave a quick glance to the receptionist that Nicole noticed immediately.

"Nicole!" Charles exclaimed. "What a surprise. Come on back. Whitney, please hold my calls."

Oh! Nicole thought, *pretty brunette has a name.*

Once, back in his office, Charles shut the door and said, "I thought I asked you to text me before stopping by my office." He went to sit behind his desk.

"I didn't know you were serious about that," Nicole replied as she perched on the edge of his desk. "I would think you would like the fact your wife wants to see you more than just at home."

Charles relaxed a little and replied, getting up, "You're right. I am grateful that I have you, Nicole. Do you want to grab a bite to eat together?"

"Yes, I do." With that, Nicole put her arm through Charles', and they left his office. As they passed the reception area, Nicole looked over her shoulder at Whitney and said, "Have a nice day, Whitney."

Whitney smirked and turned her back on the two. Charles looked straight ahead.

Nicole poured over their bank account. She was certain there was something going on between Charles and Whitney. Trish had confirmed her hunch when Nicole recalled the story of her showing up and surprising Charles for lunch.

"Oh, yes," Trish replied, "he is hiding something. You need to snoop."

Nicole looked at every entry on the online bank statement. Charles was smart. He only had cash withdrawals and bill payments shown on the statement. She was mildly shocked to see how much money they had in their checking account when she was still receiving a paltry weekly allowance.

It was only after going back three months that she found a suspicious charge. It was a bar charge at a local hotel for $16.00. She clicked on the charge, but she could only see the date and amount.

Nicole wondered when Whitney started at the agency and if this charge was somehow related.

"Charles," Nicole asked at dinner. "Your new receptionist is so sweet. When did she start with your company? Should we have her and her husband over for dinner?"

Charles about choked on his food. "What?" he asked, "Where did that come from?"

"I don't know," Nicole replied. "I just felt it was important to get to know her better since she works at your office with you and your dad all day."

Charles choked on his food and after he regained his composure, he reassured Nicole, "She is fine and has a boyfriend who is very supportive."

"Does she?" Nicole asked as Charles looked away.

Nicole wasn't going to let this issue go. If Charles was cheating on her, she would get to the bottom of the dilemma. She found out the answer when Charles' parents came over for Sunday dinner the following weekend. As Charles' father brought in the burgers, Nicole asked her father-in-law a question. "I met your new receptionist Whitney last week and she was so nice. When did she start at the agency?"

Charles' father seemed to think about the question a minute and answered, "She started about three months ago. She is the daughter of an old friend of mine. Charles has been really good about making her feel welcome."

Nicole felt sick to her stomach.

It was a couple of days later that she looked at the charge again. What would Charles be doing at a hotel bar?

Nicole brought the charge up to Trish who immediately went into super sleuth mode. "I don't think anything good is going to come with this," Trish began, "but the real question is do you want to get to the bottom of this?"

"Yes, I do," Nicole answered. "I can't keep living with this hanging over my head."

They developed a plan and decided to put it into place as soon as possible.

Nicole asked Charles when they could meet for lunch. He quickly replied," I can't meet Wednesday. I, uh, have a meeting outside of the office. But I can go to lunch Thursday."

"Sure, " Nicole responded. "It's a date."

When she told Trish what Charles had said, Trish reached over and grabbed her hand, "Wednesday, it is."

On Wednesday, Trish and Nicole parked a discreet distance from Charles' office in Trish's car.

"Maybe what he said was true," Nicole started. "Maybe he does have a meeting outside the office."

Trish didn't respond but pointed straight ahead.

There was Charles and Whitney walking to his car. He graciously opened her door for her, and he walked to his side and got in. He took a right on Main Street and Trish pulled out to follow him. Charles eventually pulled into the Mayfield Hotel and parked on the side of the building. The same hotel where Nicole had found the bar charge.

Trish pulled into a spot far enough away that they couldn't be seen.

Charles got out of the car alone and walked into the hotel. "What is he doing?" Nicole asked.

About five minutes later, Whitney got out of the car and entered the hotel lobby.

"Hold tight," Trish said as she got out of the car. "I'll be right back."

When Trish got back in the car, her face was solemn. "She went to room 115. I followed her and that's the room she went into." Trish looked at Nicole and said, "I am sorry, Nic. What are you going to do?"

"Exactly what we planned," Nicole said as she opened the passenger side door. "Exactly what we planned."

Nicole crossed the lobby and down the hallway towards the room. Outside of room 115, she took her cell phone out of her pocket and pressed Charles' phone number.

Inside the room, she heard a phone ring and recognized her ring tone on his phone. She couldn't make out what was being said, but Charles answered on the third ring.

"Hello?" he asked angrily.

Nicole hung up the phone without a word and before she could falter, she started banging on the door of room 115.

"Open the door. Open the door now!" She kept banging on the door with her fist, yelling, "Open the door, Charles, open the door now."

Nicole heard the chain slide, and after what seemed to take forever, the door opened. Charles stood there, with lipstick smeared on his face.

Nicole couldn't see Whitney, but it didn't matter. Charles looked livid and said, "Nicole, what are you doing—"

He didn't get the chance to finish. Nicole slapped him across the face as hard as she could and left him standing in the doorway with a stunned expression and her handprint on his face. Nicole didn't remember the car ride back to the office. Once back, Trish made her eat and drink something before she said, "We need to start protecting you and the kids. Let's start with your bank account."

Nicole was waiting for Charles to arrive home after work. She had taken the kids to her mother's with a promise to pick them up later. She was prepared for the confrontation and had steeled herself to whatever personality of Charles' came through the garage door. She heard the door open, and a few minutes later, there was Charles, standing in front of her. Nicole sat at the kitchen table, looking straight at him.

Time passed, and neither said a word. Suddenly, Charles was on his knees with his head in her lap, crying. "I am so sorry, Nicole. I am so sorry. Please forgive me."

Nicole was shocked; this was not what she had expected. She expected an angry and defiant man, not one crying in her lap, begging forgiveness. She was suddenly torn between her emotions. This was the man she loved and the father of her children. Should she be forgiving and try to keep her small family together, or walk away? How could she do this alone?

Nicole looked down at Charles' head in her lap. She had to give him another chance. The marriage vows were 'for better or worse', right? Nicole had a feeling this was the last time Charles would be unfaithful to her. It was probably all Whitney's fault for coming on to Charles.

All she could do was grasp his head and lift it up. She kissed his forehead and said, "Okay, okay, I forgive you, my love."

Charles kissed her hands, looked her in the eye and said, "I am so in love with you. I will never betray you again, Nicole."

Trish was less than impressed when Nicole told her the story the next day.

"Well," Trish said. "Do me a favor and don't close the bank account we set up. At least for a while, until we know this apology is legit."

Nicole reluctantly agreed but felt that Charles would stay true to his word, and that everything was going to be good again.

Nicole dropped by Charles' office later in the week and an older woman was sitting at the receptionist desk.

"Hello," Nicole said, reaching out her hand. "I am Nicole, Charles' wife. Is he in?"

"Well, aren't you so pretty?" The older woman shook her hand. "I am Madge, the new receptionist here at the company. I am an old friend of Charles' father and was so glad to get the call to come in and help." Madge leaned in closer. "Retirement wasn't for me. I wasn't meant to stay at home and watch soap operas."

They had arrived at the door to Charles' office, where, upon seeing Nicole, he broke into a big smile.

"Madge, I see you met my favorite girl. She is the love of my life." Nicole blushed. It had been a long time since Charles had been so openly affectionate to her.

Charles thanked Madge for bringing Nicole back to his office and grabbed Nicole's hand. Charles said, "Let's go to lunch, my dear. I am so glad you stopped by."

A week later, Nicole was cleaning up the dinner dishes, humming to herself as she listened to Charles and the kids outside shooting baskets and laughing. She looked out the window, memorizing the scene in front of her, wishing she could share this with Trish. She heard a phone vibrate and turned and looked at the kitchen table, where she saw Charles' phone. It vibrated again and Nicole picked it up to see who was texting him.

As she looked at the message, her heart stopped. The message said, "I miss you already! So glad we had today together. See you very soon, love. W."

Charles appeared in the kitchen as Nicole looked up with tears in her eyes. This time, it was a very different Charles.

"What are you doing? Why are you going through my phone?" Charles said angrily and grabbed the phone out of her hands.

"I wasn't going through your phone; it vibrated, and I picked it up." Nicole responded.

She looked back out the window at the kid's playing basketball.

Nicole turned around, looked at a furious Charles and said, "I want a divorce."

Brad

Nicole and Brad decided it was time for their kids to meet. They had both told their children they were dating someone. Brad's children took it much better than Nicole's, who still had wounds from the divorce and the ugly aftermath. Brad decided on a local hamburger place. As Nicole pulled up with kids in the car, she pleaded with them one last time.

"Please give Brad a chance. I really like him," Nicole said.

"Like the way you gave Dad a chance, huh?" Grace said, getting out of the car and slamming the door.

Once inside, after they were all seated around the table, Brad spoke to Ben and Grace.

"I am glad I finally got to meet you both," he started. "I knew your mom and dad when we went to high school together."

"Back in the stone age?" Grace responded.

Brad never missed a beat. "Yep. I was the bad kid, and your mom was Miss Goody Two Shoes."

Both Ben and Grace took the bait. "Tell us! Tell us!" Brad's children rolled their eyes. They obviously had heard this story before.

Nicole glanced at Brad before he started and said, "I remember some stories about you too, Mister."

Obviously, nothing gets kids more animated than hearing embarrassing stories about their parents.

"I remember at an assembly; your mom got an award for not being absent from school for all four years of high school." Brad looked around the table and laughed. "And I got the award for missing the most school days."

It wasn't long before Brad had the whole table laughing, mainly by poking fun at himself. Nicole saw Grace speaking to Brad's daughter about some new app on her phone and Brad was talking to Ben about soccer.

"Of course, I didn't play soccer, but I have a guy at work who does private coaching. Let me know if you want his number."

When Brad glanced at Nicole, she smiled and mouthed the words, "Thank you."

"So," Brad asked the table, "can we do this once a week, so we can get to know each other better?" Brad elbowed Ben and smiled at Grace.

"Because I don't think your mom is going to quit chasing me around town. Isn't that right, Miss Goody Two Shoes?" Brad laughed.

The table roared with laughter and the response was, "Yes!" and "Next time, let's get pizza."

On the way out, Brad grabbed Nicole's hand and whispered in her ear, "I think it went well. Don't you?"

Charles

Nicole packed up the kids and herself and headed to her mother's house the night she found the text on Charles' phone. The kids cried and were confused as to why they were going to their grandmother's house. Charles didn't help with the situation. He followed her from room to room, shouting." You don't have to do this, Nicole, you are overreacting." He reached out and grabbed her arm. WIth the kids out of sight, Nicole shoved Charles back into the wall. She had never as much as touched him in anger and he was shocked.

"Don't you ever touch me again," Nicole said quietly. "I am done with you, and I am done with this marriage. "

"You can't be serious?" Charles asked. "I hold your life in my hands. You will never make it without me."

Nicole laughed at Charles. "I can't wait to try. Now, get out of my way."

Nicole arrived at her mom's house later, with suitcases and two distraught kids. Nicole's mother opened the door and hugged each one of them.

"I have rooms ready for you all." She hugged Nicole tightly and whispered in her ear, "I never did care for that creep you married. I will help you every way I can," and ushered them into the house. Nicole's mom put her in her old room and the kids in the rooms down the hall. Both kids were shell-shocked and went to their rooms and shut the door.

Nicole's mom sat on the edge of Nicole's bed and held her hand while tears streamed down Nicole's face. "Oh, my sweet girl. I am so sorry," Nicole's mom said as she wiped away her daughter's tears. "You can stay here as long as you want."

Nicole was grateful for her mother's generosity and open invitation. "Oh, Mom," Nicole said as she wrapped her arms around her mother. "How could he do this to us?"

Nicole called in sick to work the next day and let the kids skip school so they could all take a day off. She called Trish and told her what had happened and why she wasn't at work.

"I would have loved to have seen his face when you walked out," Trish whispered into the phone. "But seriously, how are the kids doing?"

"Not well," Nicole replied. "I don't want to go into detail with the children about why I left their father."

"Well, then don't," Trish said. "You don't want this to be a 'he said, she said' argument. Tell them you grew apart and that they will always be a part of their dad's' life. You just aren't going to be married any longer."

Nicole put her head in her hands. "I don't even know a divorce attorney or where to start."

"Let me take care of that, " Trish replied. "I think my husband has some lawyer friends. You just take care of you."

Nicole and the kids sat around the dinner table later the next day, picking at the food on their plates while Nicole's mom kept up a conversation, mainly to herself. As she leaned over to pick up the kid's' plates, Nicole stopped her and said, "Mom, the kids can clear their own plates, you don't need to wait on us. We are grateful we are staying here, so we will help you."

"Maybe *you* are glad for us to be here," Grace shouted and shoved her chair back from the table. "I want to be home, in my house, in my room. Not here with you," and she ran up the stairs and slammed the door to her bedroom.

Nicole's eyes filled with tears. She got up and started helping her mom clean up the dinner dishes.

Ben reached out for Nicole's arm. "Mom, you are going to have to tell us why we all left home and what's going to happen to us." He spoke quietly. "We deserve to know the truth."

Later, Nicole knocked on the door to Grace's room. "Can I come in, Grace?" Nicole heard sniffling and a small voice say, "I guess."

Nicole opened the door and slipped into the room. She sat on the edge on the bed and rubbed Grace's back. "Can I talk to you?" Grace glanced sideways at Nicole and nodded.

"I love you. Your dad loves you. I love your dad too, but we are at a place where we need to take some time apart," Nicole said. "I told your brother this just a bit ago. You will still be able to see your dad anytime you want to, and even stay the night at our house, but I am going to be staying here at Grandmas for a while."

Gracie sat up and hugged her knees to her chest. Tears rolled down her cheeks. "I just don't want to be one of those kids with divorced parents.

I never thought that it would happen to us."

Nicole held Grace's hand and quietly said, "Me, either."

Brad

"My friend has a cabin in the mountains not far from here," Brad said quietly. "He said it's free this weekend if you want to get away."

Nicole looked up Brad, trying to gauge if he was serious. By the look on his face, he most certainly was serious. Nicole chewed on her lower lip. The physical attraction between them was red hot, and lately, all they had the opportunity to do was kiss in the car whenever the kids weren't looking. This weekend, both sets of kids would be with their other parents, which presented the perfect time for the two of them to have some private time.

The truth of the matter was that Nicole was terrified. She had only been with Charles, and the passion she felt for Brad didn't resemble anything she had experienced with Charles. Still, Nicole worried. Would she be enough for Brad? Would she know what to do? She knew Brad had a lot more experience with women than she had when she was with Charles.

The worry must have shown on her face because Brad suddenly grabbed her hands and said, "Look at me, babe, look at me now."

Nicole looked into Brad's eyes, the eyes that lit up when she came into a room, the eyes that she was falling in love with.

"I know you have to be… um… nervous, I guess," Brad said. "I am nervous too." Nicole laughed.

"No, I am serious," Brad said, kissing her hands that he held so tightly. "I have never been with anyone like you."

Nicole arched her eyebrows.

"Gosh, I am making a mess of this," Brad swore. "Okay, here it is, straight up. I know you have only been with your husband, and you know I haven't exactly been with just one person. But I am so into you, I want us to spend some time together. I will be respectful of you, and if you say no, that's okay. I just want us to spend some time away together and see what we can become."

Tears sprang into Nicole's eyes. Never had she heard anything so beautiful.

"Yes," Nicole said as she leaned in and kissed Brad. "Let's go to the mountains this weekend."

When Brad had picked her up and was loading her bag, Nicole's mom leaned in and winked at Nicole. To say she was not nervous, was an understatement, but this was the man whom she loved, and she wanted to please him, but due to her experience, she wasn't sure she knew exactly what to do to make that happen.

They laughed as they unloaded the car and opened the door to the cabin. "It's beautiful!" exclaimed Nicole. "What a view!" she added, stepping out onto the back porch.

"Yes," Brad said, wrapping his arms around her. "You are beautiful." Nicole playfully swatted his arms, but her heart was pounding. She was in love. After unpacking the groceries and the snacks Nicole's mother had sent with them, it was time for just the two of them. Brad looked around the cabin and then put his arms around Nicole and kissed her.

"How about a little hike?" he asked. "Are you up for it?"

"Sure," Nicole replied. "Let's go!"

Brad led the way and they found a path where they could walk side by side while holding hands. The weather was starting to change, and the leaves were beginning to turn colors. Brad pointed out trees and foliage and began telling Nicole about the plants.

"How do you know all about this?" Nicole asked.

"Well, it might have looked like I was goofing off in high school, but I loved science class, especially botany. I made an A in all of my science classes, which was funny because I made C's and D's in my other classes. Old Principal Tucker could never figure that out," He laughed.

Nicole laughed too. "That's what we all get for believing in stereotypes. I mean, everyone thought I had the perfect marriage. The neighbors were shocked when we split up."

Brad stopped and looked directly at her.

"Babe, don't bring him along today, okay? Let it just be you and me," Brad whispered.

Nicole smiled and nodded her head. She wrapped her arms around Brad and held on to him tightly and he held her back. He leaned down and kissed the top of her head. They stood there together, enjoying the sounds of nature and the feel of each other.

Dinner was wonderful. Brad grilled steaks while Nicole threw together a salad. They ate dinner out on the deck and laughed while they ate and drank red wine. Lots of red wine. As Nicole was cleaning up the kitchen, Brad called out, "Babe! You have got to come see this sunset."

Nicole dried her hands and joined Brad on the deck. Together, they stood watching the sun set over a masterpiece of the autumn trees. Brad pulled Nicole closer and whispered, "Life is so much better with you in it, Nicole."

Nicole turned, put her arms around Brad's neck and began to kiss him. The red wine gave her courage and a yearning for something more. Brad looked down at her and raised his eyebrows. Nicole gave him a sultry smile and took his hand to lead him in the house. As soon as they got to the bedroom, clothes went flying and they toppled onto the bed.

Much later, both were lying side by side, trying to catch their breath. Nicole looked over at Brad as he wrapped her in his arms.

"Damn, Nicole, you about killed me," Brad teased.

Nicole sat up and looked down at him, tracing her fingers over his face.

"And," Brad added," I can't think of a better way to die. Want to try and kill me again?"

Nicole smiled and whispered, "Yes."

Charles

"Let me in this house!" Nicole screamed at the closed door. "I know you are in there."

Nicole continued to bang on the front door of her old house until the neighbor next door came to the backyard fence and called out, "Nicole, can I help you with something?"

Nicole looked at the woman and went blank for her name. Was it Sarah, or Theresa?

As if the woman sensed her confusion, she said, "I'm Sarah from next door. Do you want to come in for a cup of tea?"

Nicole smoothed her hair and straightened her jacket. "Yes, a cup of tea would be great." Nicole walked to the fence and followed Sarah into her kitchen. She glanced around the house and admired the homey feel of the furnishings. This was the kind of furniture she had always wanted for the home next door, but her suggestions were always met with another idea. Charles' idea.

As Sarah set down a cup of tea in front of Nicole, Nicole glanced up at her and said, "You must think I am crazy, over at my house banging on the door like a mad woman."

"Well," Sarah began, "I was wondering where you and the kids were. There hasn't been much activity next door, and I was beginning to get worried."

Nicole took a sip of her tea and looked at Sarah.

Nicole started her explanation. "The kids and I moved out a couple weeks ago."

Sarah looked shocked. She said, "We always thought you were the perfect family."

Nicole chuckled. "You have no idea what it was like in that house."

Sarah reached over and took Nicole's hand and squeezed gently. "You can talk to me," she said softly.

With that comment, Nicole began telling Sarah everything. From high school to their marriage and how Charles controlled every minute of her life.

"I even got an allowance each week," Nicole said. "And my spending was monitored daily. I would walk in the door and he would be asking why I spent so much at the grocery store."

"Don't you work too?" Sarah asked.

"Yes, I do," Nicole replied. "My checks were direct-deposited, and he was in charge of the checkbook. I have never paid a bill in my life."

"Wow, I had no idea," Sarah was shaking her head.

"Yes. Perfect on the outside and so dark on the inside," Nicole said. "The kids never saw his controlling behavior, so they both think I have left their dad for no reason. All I want to do is get in the house and get some things for the children and myself. And I think he changed the locks, the jerk," Nicole put her head in her hands. "I can't believe this is my life."

Sarah scooted her chair closer to Nicole and whispered, "I could text you when I see his car pull in the driveway. That way, you can get what is yours and get the heck out of that house."

Nicole stared at Sarah in shock. "Why would you help me? You don't even know me, and I have been a terrible neighbor."

Sarah looked at her and said, "My father was just like your husband, and he made my mom's life miserable, but she never left him. I couldn't get out of that house fast enough when I was old enough. He died about ten years ago and my mom is a new woman. Mom didn't deserve to be treated the way she was, and neither do you. That's why I want to help you."

Tears poured down Nicole's cheeks. "Thank you!" she whispered.

Two days later, Nicole got the text. She kissed the kids and told them she would be back soon. Nicole pulled in the driveway and saw Charles' car parked in the back. She glanced over at Sarah's porch and saw Sarah give her a little wave at the window and then she disappeared.

Nicole took a deep breath and went to the front door. "Might as well put on a show for the neighbors," Nicole said to herself. She tried the doorknob and found it was locked. She tried her key, and it didn't fit.

"Just as I thought." Nicole raised her fist and started banging on the front door.

"Charles! Let me in this house! Open the door and let me into this house now!" Nicole banged on the door and kept yelling over and over, "Let me in this house. Your children need their clothes, and you can't keep me out of my house."

Charles yanked open the front door with an incredulous look on his face. "What the heck do you think you are doing?" he asked as he glanced around the cul-de-sac.

"Let me in this house. Our house," Nicole demanded. "The kids need their clothes and I need a few things of my own." She tried to move past Charles into the house, but he put his arm across the door jamb to block her path.

"Well, let me think," he snarled. "I wasn't the one who packed up and left, was I? So why would I let you in *my* house?" His face was a mask of anger, and for a moment, Nicole thought about backing down, but then she realized she had always backed down to Charles, and today was a new day.

"Let me in the house right now!" Nicole yelled. "This is my house, too, and you can't keep me out." She attempted to push by Charles but he held firm, blocking her path.

"Damn you, Charles," Nicole yelled. "You have and will always be a bully."

Again, she tried to push past him, and he grabbed her arm and twisted it. Nicole yelped in pain and tried to wrestle her arm away. "Let me go," Nicole yelled even louder. "You are hurting me. I just want to get clothes for the kids. I won't get any of my things. Does that make you feel better?" she asked.

Charles twisted her arm harder until she cried out in pain.

"Sir, I suggest you take your hands off that woman right now," a voice stated behind Charles and Nicole. Both turned to see a police officer standing outside his cruiser in the driveway. Neither had heard him pull up. Nicole turned to see Sarah standing on her porch with her arms crossed and a concerned look on her face.

Charles let go of Nicole's arm and put his hands up in the air. "Officer," Charles started, "we are having a little disagreement, you know, a private disagreement between a couple. We don't need your help. Thank you."

"Well," the police officer said, walking toward the front porch. "I saw you put your hands on this woman and witnessed her cry out in pain, so now, it is my problem. Step back, sir."

Charles challenged, "Do you have a search warrant? This is my property!"

The police officer smiled and put his hand on the revolver on his belt and countered, "Do I need to get one, or are you going to let this lady in this house?"

Charles was livid. "She left me. She took our kids and left me. I don't have to let her in this house!" Charles sputtered.

The police officer approached closer, with his hand still on his revolver.

"Is her name on the deed to this house?" the police officer asked.

"What?" Charles asked. "Of course, it is."

"Then you let her in," the police officer responded. "Or you go to jail."

About this time, another police cruiser pulled up and the second police officer got out of his car.

Nicole glanced around the cul-de-sac and saw curtains being pulled apart to get a better look at what was going on at the normally quiet residence. As much as Nicole liked seeing Charles put in his place, she knew she needed to step in. Nicole stepped in front of Charles and looked him straight in his eyes.

"Charles," she whispered, "just let me in the house to get some clothes, and I will leave. We don't want to make a scene, do we?"

With that comment, Charles glanced around the neighborhood and quickly came to his senses.

"Come on inside and get what you need," he said as he stepped aside and let her in the front door.

"We are fine. You can leave now," Charles called out to the police officer.

"I think we will just wait here until your wife comes back out," the first police officer said as he leaned back on his cruiser.

Inside, Nicole went straight to the storage closet and pulled out two suitcases. She proceeded to the children's room and started packing. Charles stood at the bedroom door watching her. Nicole didn't let that stop her and packed the essentials the children needed. After she was finished, she walked past Charles and he grabbed her arm.

"Nicole," Charles started. "Please don't do this. I promise I will change. It was her fault. She wouldn't leave me alone. She kept flirting with me at work and texting me stuff." Nicole tuned him out as she gathered her toiletries from the bathroom. She reached into the dresser drawers and pulled out everything she could get her hands on. As she opened the closet, she realized she was going to have to leave some of her clothing, as she couldn't take everything today. She grabbed a bag and started putting shoes in it.

As she turned to leave the bedroom, Charles began pleading. "Please don't leave me, Nicole. I can't do this without you." Charles' voice wavered. Nicole glanced at Charles and thought she saw tears in his eyes, but the voice in her head warned her that Charles was a great actor and he had played her their entire marriage. But Nicole thought, she did need help getting the luggage out to the car and there was the possibility she would need back inside the house.

She turned back to Charles. "Stop it, Charles," she began. "You cheated on me and that's devastating. It's not something I can just easily forget about. I need time to heal. Let me have some time please?"

Charles paused and then said, "Of course, of course. I am here waiting for you when you and the kids want to come back. I miss you, Nicole." Charles attempted to hug Nicole, but she stepped back.

"Can you help me with the bags?" Nicole asked. Now that he thought he had Nicole right where he wanted her, Charles was more than accommodating. He grabbed the luggage and helped Nicole load it into the trunk of her car. He even waved at the police officer who was standing by his patrol car talking to Sarah. Nicole got into her car before Charles attempted another hug. He leaned on the car's window edge and asked, "When can I see you and the kids again?"

"I will be in touch, Charles. I know the kids want to see you. Take care of yourself," That was all Nicole could think of what to say at that moment. Charles stood in the driveway waving as Nicole backed down the driveway. For a split second, she thought about stopping the car and running back to him and putting this all behind them, but then she remembered the text message.

Nicole waved back and said under her breath, "It will be a cold day in hell before I move back into that house," and she drove away.

Later that night at her mom's, Nicole got a text message from Sarah. It read, 'If you need my brother, the policeman, to stop by next time you need something from your house, just let me know. You hang in there, girl!'

Nicole smiled and texted back, 'Thank you, Sarah.'

Trish laughed so hard when Nicole told her about the incident at the house with Charles and her neighbor's police officer brother that people looked over the cubicle at her.

"She must have texted him after she texted me Charles was home," Nicole explained and couldn't help giggling herself.

"Did you get everything you needed?" Trish asked.

"No, I didn't," Nicole explained. "I was trying not to escalate the situation, and by doing that, I forgot some of the kids' items I needed."

Trish pulled out a pad and pen. "Let's start making a list so you won't forget what you need the next time you have to go over to Chuck's place."

The next time Nicole texted Charles about coming over to pick up more items, he suggested Friday night and asked if she could bring the children.

"Sure," Nicole texted back. That way, the children could keep Charles busy so she could focus on packing without him following her around the house.

Nicole and the kids arrived on Friday night and knocked on the back door.

Charles opened the door and said, "Welcome home, everyone!"

Nicole stepped inside and froze. Charles had set the table for all of them, and food was on the table.

"I thought we could have dinner as a family," he boasted proudly. Nicole forced a smile when the children looked back at her and she nodded yes, but she knew exactly what Charles was up to. He was going to play the family back together card, but

Nicole wasn't going to take the bait. After a few bites, Nicole excused herself and went upstairs to pack some clothes from her closet. As she was putting her clothes in the suitcase, Charles popped his head around the door.

"What are you doing?" he asked. "I am trying to have a family dinner and you leave as soon as we sit down." Nicole turned back to her clothes closet and continued pulling out clothes.

"Charles," Nicole replied. "I know what you're doing. You're trying to make it seem like there is nothing wrong between us by having dinner for us. We both know we have issues in this marriage."

She could see Charles was getting frustrated with her, so she tried a different approach.

"Charles, dear," Nicole began. "The kids have been dying to see you, it's all they have been talking about this week. Why don't you go spend time with them and I'll be down in a minute, and we can all have dessert together?" Truth be told, the kids hadn't mentioned their father much, but Nicole knew that Charles would fall for the compliment, and he did.

Nicole didn't know how much longer she could manipulate Charles to let her take items out of the house and she couldn't go on living with her mother. It was time to get her own place and try to figure out what she was going to do with her life. She glanced around and realized she was going to have to start fresh for any furniture and beds.

Charles would not let her take any of those items with her; she knew that for a fact.

"Mom!" the kids yelled. "We are waiting for you to have ice cream. Come down!"

Nicole took one more look around the bedroom she had shared with Charles all these years. 'Time for a change,' a voice said in her head, and she knew it to be true. She grabbed her suitcases and headed down for ice cream.

It was time for Nicole and the kids to move out of her mother's house. Nicole's mom protested, but both Claire and Nicole knew it was time. The small house had been great for Nicole's parents, but with Nicole and two teenagers, everyone felt on top of each other. When Nicole said she was looking for a house, but didn't know how she could get a loan because Charles had all the credit, Nicole's mom said, "I will pay the down payment for the house and you can pay the house payment."

Nicole attempted to protest, but it was the only way until she got a better credit score. When Gracie and Ben overheard the conversation about Nicole buying a house, Gracie exploded.

"How can you do this to us?" she shrieked. "How can you do this to Dad?" And she flew out of the room with a door slamming a few seconds later.

Ben shoved his hands in his pockets and looked at the floor.

"Ben," Nicole asked, "do you have something to say to me?" Ben shrugged his shoulders and quietly said, "We just thought you and Dad were trying to work things out. I don't think buying a house for us is working things out, you know?" With that, he walked to the kitchen door and stepped outside.

Nicole felt terrible and looked back at her mother.

"Stop right now, Nicole Ann," her mother said. "I wish you would have listened to us when you wanted to marry Charles so young."

"Mom! Stop!" Nicole tried to get up and walk away.

Her mom grabbed her arm and said, "Sit down, now."

Nicole's mother never raised her voice, so Nicole did as she was told. "I know you loved Charles, and you have two beautiful children from that marriage. But, Nicole, based on what you told me, I believe your marriage is over. You are going to have to be strong for your children, or Charles will turn them against you. You are their mother; start acting like one."

With that comment, her mom got up and left Nicole in the kitchen alone.

Nicole wished she had never brought the kids back into the living room to discuss the move. Gracie was yelling about not wanting to move to another house, and Ben kept telling Gracie to quiet down.

Finally, Nicole stood up and said, "Enough!" Both children went silent. Nicole took a deep breath and said, "I want to talk about this as a family team."

Gracie snapped back, "If this was a family team, Dad would be here." She crossed her arms in front of her chest. Nicole didn't let the outburst persuade her to give up on the conversation.

"Guys," Nicole said, "we can't continue to stay here with Grandma. She has been gracious to let us be here this long, but we need more room."

Gracie stood up and made a comment under her breath about having room at the old house with her father when Nicole said, "Enough, Gracie! Either be part of the discussion or stay quiet."

Gracie sat down on the sofa but looked away from her mother.

Nicole started talking. "I want to stay in your same school district so that you both won't need to change schools. I don't know what kind of house I will be able to afford since it will be just me making the house payment. I would really appreciate your help with me picking out a new place to live."

Ben quietly asked, "So, Mom, are you saying that we won't be moving back to Dad's house anytime soon?"

Nicole reached over and grabbed his hand and replied, "No, Ben, I won't be moving back into your father's house anytime soon, but you both will be seeing him on a regular basis, I promise you."

Gracie shook her head while tears streamed down her cheeks. Nicole wanted to reach out, but she knew Gracie, and she needed time to process the information.

Ben said, "I have an idea. Why don't we look at a condo? You know my friend Jeff. Well, when his mom split from his dad; she bought a condo. When

I was over there, she said it had room enough for everyone and no yard work. Let's be honest, Mom." Ben grinned shyly. "You are not a yard work mom."

With that comment, Gracie snorted and then covered her smile with her sleeve.

Nicole glanced at both of her children and felt so proud of them. "Okay!" Nicole reached out for her children and surprisingly they both came to her side. "A condo it is for us. Let's start looking tomorrow!"

Ben got the name of his friend Jeff's mothers' condo, and they all went to check out the complex the next day. There wasn't an open unit available at the complex, which was a little too expensive for Nicole in the first place.

When Nicole was telling Trish about her decision to purchase a condo, Trish answered and said, "I have just the place for you!"

As usual, Trish came through with a condo Nicole could afford and was just inside the boundaries of the children's school district. It wasn't brand new but had good bones. This was the first home that Nicole owned herself on her own and she was very proud of herself.

On moving day, Nicole made it an adventure for the children to bring in their meager belongings and place their furniture any way they wanted it in their rooms. They had to share a bathroom, which Gracie fussed about, and Nicole responded, "At least you have your own room."

Gracie mumbled something but seemed in a better mood when she could hang posters on her bedroom wall. Charles had never allowed any posters in her room as he didn't like any holes in "his" house walls. Today, Nicole didn't care. She knew you could plug holes, just like she had done in her life.

Nicole stood in her bedroom. It was small, but it was all hers. "Knock, knock," Nicole heard from the hallway. It was her mother with two pizza boxes in her hands. "Who wants pizza? That's what you're supposed to eat when you move, right?"

The children were excited to see their grandmother and led her to their rooms to show off their handiwork. As usual, Nicole's mom was excited to see what they had done and praised their decorating.

"What about you, my dear?" Nicole's mom asked as she glanced into Nicole's bedroom. "This is the most boring bedroom I have ever seen."

Nicole laughed at her mom's bluntness and replied, "It is just the way I want it to be. Come on, Mom, let's go eat pizza."

Brad

Nicole and Brad were out to lunch when he suddenly asked, "Are you dating anyone else?"

Nicole's fork paused halfway to her mouth as she looked at Brad and began to chuckle.

"What's so funny?" Brad asked, with a mischievous smile on his face.

"I can barely make time to see you, take care of the kids and work. I have no time to date anyone else, and I don't want to date anyone else," Nicole replied.

"Good," Brad responded and dug into his sandwich.

Nicole put her fork down and asked, "I thought we had already discussed this. Have you changed your mind? Are you-?

"Am I what?" Brad responded.

"Dating anyone else besides me?" Nicole asked quietly. Her old insecurities were rushing into her head as much as she tried to push them down.

Of course, Brad had a mouth full of his sandwich so Nicole had to wait until he chewed, swallowed and took a drink of his water.

"What was the question again?" Brad asked and ducked when Nicole tossed her napkin at him.

"Okay, here's the thing," Brad started, leaning across the table toward Nicole. "I am done dating anyone else but you. You are all I think about. I think about you when I wake up in the morning and you are my last thought before I go to sleep. There is no one else I want to spend time with and I just wanted to check and make sure you felt the same way about being just with me."

Nicole eyes filled with tears. Brad sighed. "I always seem to make you cry. What's up with that?"

Nicole wiped her eyes and looked at Brad. "I am not crying; those are tears of joy because you say such nice things to me. Sometimes I can't believe this is happening to me."

Brad swore under his breath and said, "That ex of yours really did a job on you."

He took her hand. "I will spend every day proving to you that you deserve everything that's good and positive because you are the sweetest person I have ever met, and I want to see you smile. I love your smile. And I love you, Nicole."

Of course, Nicole's eyes filled up again and she giggled.

Brad laughed, too, and commented, "You are even more beautiful when you are crying. Thank goodness you aren't an ugly crier; I couldn't handle that." Brad kept his word, and whether it was a text message, or a flower left on her front porch, he made it his job to help Nicole feel loved and more confident in their relationship.

Charles

Nicole was catching up with Trish on Monday morning at work, over coffee, when a young man knocked on her door.

"Can I speak to Nicole Chapman please?"

This young man barely looked old enough to vote, let alone flirt with them.

"I am," Nicole replied. "What can I do for you?"

"I have something for you," he responded and pulled a large envelope out of his backpack. "Here you go."

He handed it to Nicole. Nicole reached out and took the envelope from his hands. "What's in here?" she asked, still smiling from the encounter with the young man.

"Nicole Chapman, you have been served. Have a nice day." With that response, he was gone.

Nicole looked at Trish and asked, "Served?"

Trish looked straight at Nicole and said, "The douche bag husband of yours is serving you divorce papers at work. What a loser."

Nicole was shocked. She had spoken to Charles briefly over the weekend about childcare arrangements for the upcoming week and he never mentioned he was filing for divorce.

Nicole became angry. This was just like Charles pulling a stunt like this so everything was his idea. He had her served at work to embarrass her. Luckily, only Trish saw the interaction. Nicole read the paperwork and laughed out loud. Trish leaned over her desk. "Do tell," she whispered.

"He is divorcing me for spousal abandonment and wants joint custody of the children. And absolutely no alimony. Trish, how can I do this?" Nicole asked, crestfallen.

Trish walked over to Nicole's desk and put her arm around her shoulders. "Here's how you do it, " Trish said quietly. "Her name is Carolyn Matthews. And she will take ole Chuck to the cleaners."

Sitting in Carolyn Matthews' law office waiting area was completely intimidating. As Nicole looked around the all-white office, she had a thought that the white leather sofa she was sitting on cost more than her monthly condo payment. But, according to Trish, she was the best divorce attorney in town.

When a young man came to take Nicole back for her meeting, she took a deep breath and followed him to a glass conference room with, of course, white leather chairs. Shortly afterwards, Carolyn Matthews entered the room with the young man following close behind. "Good morning, Mrs. Chapman. I am Carolyn Matthews, and I am so excited to meet with you." If everything in the office was white, Carolyn was a blast of color, jet-black hair piled high on her head, red business suit, Chanel scarf and sky-high stilettos. Nicole immediately felt very underdressed.

"Would you like something to drink?" Carolyn asked after the introduction, and they were seated.

"Water would be fine," Nicole replied. "Thank you for seeing me so quickly. I wasn't expected to be served divorce papers. Charles and I never officially discussed filing for divorce."

Without looking up from her laptop that she was furiously typing on with long, manicured nails, Carolyn said, "No one ever is prepared to be served. Jacob, two waters please."

The young man, Jacob, immediately went out of the room and returned quickly with two glasses of water.

"Thank you, Jacob. That will be all for now," Carolyn said, and Jacob left the room, pulling the door shut behind himself. Nicole was in awe of Carolyn's confident demeanor.

"Let's get started," Carolyn began, pushing the laptop to the side and placing a legal pad and pen in front of herself. "I read the information you sent over." Carolyn looked Nicole directly in the eyes. "But I want to know more. Take me all the way back to the beginning of your relationship with Charles Chapman."

Nicole started with the first time she met Charles. When she finished the whole story, she was depleted. She dabbed at the corners of her eyes with the tissue Carolyn had provided during the time she was talking. Carolyn took pages of notes while Nicole was talking, but now was looking out the conference room window with a pensive look on her face.

Nicole asked, "Ms. Mathews?"

"It's Carolyn. I am your lawyer. We are on a first name basis now," Carolyn replied, looking down at her notes.

"Carolyn, honestly, I am concerned I won't be able to afford you," Nicole said. "Your furniture is nicer than anything I have in my condo."

Carolyn let out a loud laugh. "It hasn't always been like this. When I got out of law school, I was deep in debt and took the first job I was offered." Carolyn looked around the conference room as if seeing it for the first time. "I got to this point because I am good at what I do. Now, let's talk about fees."

Nicole braced herself for the worst.

"Can you afford a $500 retainer fee for me to be your lawyer?" Carolyn asked.

"Yes, I can afford that," Nicole replied. "But what about the rest of the cost of the divorce? I don't know how long Charles will drag this out."

Carolyn leaned close to Nicole and replied, "Oh, he isn't going to drag this out for long, Nicole. I know exactly the game he and his attorney are playing. I see it all the time. And as for the cost of the proceedings, honey, Charles will be covering all your costs. That's going to be taken care of at his end. That's what I do and that's why it was a good idea to come see me." Carolyn started gathering her notes together.

"I don't even know who his lawyer is," Nicole said quietly.

"I do," Carolyn responded. "It's part of public record. His name is Daniel Tucker. And guess what? I used to work with Dan and he taught me everything I know. But here's the best part." Carolyn had a wide grin on her face and leaned into Nicole.

"He is good, but, Nicole, I am better."

And with that, Nicole held out her hand, "Carolyn, you are officially my divorce attorney."

Carolyn shook her hand and replied, "You made a good decision. I am going to take good care of you, Nicole."

Carolyn had given Nicole a list of things she needed to do while the divorce proceedings were moving forward, and one was not talking with Charles on the phone.

"Everything is text messages from now on," Carolyn had instructed her. "And keep every text from him, especially the nasty ones. I can use them when the case goes before the judge."

As Nicole left Carolyn's office, she felt her phone vibrate. She looked down and saw a text message from Charles.

"Did you get my delivery the other day?" he asked with a winking emoji.

Nicole shook her head and simply responded with the text, "Yes."

A minute later, Charles let go with a barrage of threats and insults, stating she wasn't going to get anything from him as the marriage was and had always been a sham. Normally, Nicole would have deleted the hurtful words, but today, she smiled and slipped her phone back in her purse.

"Carolyn will love to read that message." Nicole smiled and headed back to work.

Following Carolyn's advice proved to be gas on the fire for Charles and the beginning of his undoing. When Nicole didn't respond to his text messages or phone calls, he became unglued. On a call with Carolyn, after Nicole had sent her screen shots of the text messages from Charles, Carolyn made the comment, "Nicole, I think we need to consider a restraining order against Charles."

"What?" Nicole gasped. "He has never hurt me or the children, and I don't think he would."

"Nicole," Carolyn began. "Abuse is not always physical. What Charles is doing to you now, and has throughout your marriage, is psychological abuse, and that can go deeper that physical abuse because it makes you feel you aren't good enough. And let me be clear, you are good enough and you deserve a happy life, free from negative comments from a man you once loved."

Nicole was quiet and whispered, "I just don't know, Carolyn."

"I'll tell you what," Carolyn said. "Let me send him a letter that he is to cease any communication immediately, either verbal or in print with you unless it's regarding the children. He can communicate any wishes to his lawyer who can then reach out to me." Carolyn paused. " We will see how he reacts to the letter, and if something does happen, we move forward. Agreed?"

Nicole closed her eyes and whispered, "Yes."

Brad

Brad and Nicole were spending as much time together as they could find. One day, Brad was sitting out on his back porch with his best friend Tim and they both were watching Nicole and Penny, Tim's wife, set the picnic table for dinner.

"Who would have ever thought you would be in love with a girl from your high school?" Tim laughed as he sipped his beer.

"I know, right?" Brad responded. "But this relationship is different from any other one. It's just so easy to be with Nicole. I have a hard time explaining, but it's like we were meant to be together."

"Wow!" Tim said. "I never took you to be a hopeless romantic. How serious are you about this lady?"

"Pretty serious, I would say," Brad replied.

"Are you 'marriage' serious?" Tim asked quietly.

Brad shifted in his chair. "I don't know the answer to that question yet. We both initially said we would never get married again."

"Well, bud, if you are as serious as you say, you might not want to let this lady get away," Tim responded.

Brad thought for a minute and took a swig of beer. "You might be on to something there, Tim. You might be right. I don't want to lose her to anyone."

Brad got up out of his chair and went to plant a kiss on Nicole's cheek. "I love you, Nic," he whispered in her ear.

Nicole looked at Brad, slightly amused by this sudden show of affection. "I love you, too, Brad. I love you more each day," Nicole whispered back. Brad smiled; he knew exactly what he was going to do.

"The smile reminds me of the cat who swallowing the canary," Nicole jokingly replied.

"Meow!" Brad said and walked back to where Tim was seated. He needed a partner in crime.

Charles

"Quiet in my courtroom. Quiet." The judge banged her gavel on her desk. "Counsel, approach the bench, right now." Carolyn and Daniel Tucker eyed each other and approached the judge, each trying to get in front of the judge first.

"Your Honor," Daniel began, with the haughty attitude that made his reputation as a divorce lawyer popular with his clients, but not this judge.

Judge Rosemary Fowler covered her microphone and leaned forward and said, "Shut up, Tucker. Shut up."

Daniel looked shocked and his mouth dropped open. Obviously, it had been a very long time since anyone had told Daniel Tucker to shut up. Judge

Fowler looked at Carolyn and said, "And that goes for you, too, Carolyn."

Both Carolyn and Daniel stood quietly before the judge as their clients, back at the individual tables, strained to hear any of the conversation.

"I will not have this commotion in my courtroom, do you both hear me? Since your clients couldn't even meet halfway in mediation and can't agree on anything, I will not have this courtroom turned into a circus trying to get these two people divorced, am I understood?"

"Yes, Your Honor," both attorneys said in unison.

"Good," Judge Fowler said. "Now, go back to your tables and let's get this case completed so I can move on to more crap cases today." She banged her gavel again.

Carolyn went back to her table, where Nicole waited with bated breath. Carolyn smiled and whispered in her ear, "All is good." Carolyn had initially been confident in getting a woman judge for the divorce proceedings, she told Nicole, but she also knew Judge Fowler was a no-nonsense judge who wouldn't put up with any shenanigans, and that was evident as ever.

"So," Judge Fowler said to the courtroom, "let's try this again."

Daniel stood and started his speech, "Your Honor, we would like you to reconsider Mrs. Chapman's request for alimony and child support."

The whole court could hear the sigh from Judge Fowler's bench. In the end, Nicole ended up with a modest amount of child support, very little alimony and all her lawyers' fees paid by Charles. That was the best win of it all. She was so tired of sitting in the courtroom listening to the lawyers go back and forth, she was ready to take the final offer Carolyn received from Charles' lawyers.

"I think we got a decent deal," Carolyn said to Nicole as they were packing up the trial materials. "Especially when he gets my bill." She laughed and winked at Nicole.

Nicole was exhausted. All she wanted to do was go home, order the kids a pizza and disappear into her bathroom for a hot bath and a large glass of wine, so when her cell phone vibrated, she automatically answered, "Hello?"

"Well, well. You certainly got a lot more out of me than I thought you deserved, but in the end, I told Daniel to go easy on you." Charles sounded like he'd had a few drinks.

"Charles?" Nicole asked as she stopped dead in her tracks. "What are you calling me for?" She glanced nervously around the parking structure, hoping he wasn't going to pop out from behind a car.

"I just wanted to say hi and see if you and the kids want to go out for ice cream later?" Charles asked.

Nicole couldn't believe her ears. "Charles, we just spent the last three days arguing about childcare, child support and holidays, and you want to go get ice cream?" Nicole asked.

"Yes," Charles answered. "Just because we are divorced, doesn't mean we can't do things together as a family. Lots of couples successfully co-parent."

Nicole held back a chuckle. Charles couldn't co-parent if he tried, he was simply too selfish to entertain doing anything that wasn't his idea.

"No, Charles, I am not going out for ice cream with you tonight or anytime soon. We are divorced. Did you not hear the judge? We are no longer married or a couple. I think we need to be cordial for the kids' sakes, but I don't intend on going out with you anytime in the near future." Nicole had reached her car and got in and locked her door.

"Daniel said you would be like this, taking the breakup hard. He said women often feel the victim afterwards," Charles snarled.

Nicole started her car. "I am not a victim, Charles. I am free. Free of you." And with that statement, Nicole hung up on the call and started the car. She was free, so why did she feel so confined?

One year later

Nicole was watching TV in bed and munching on a bag of potato chips. She spent a lot of time in her room: it was just easier that way, so the kids could have the living room with the TV and have more space than just their rooms. If by the evidence of how much she ran them here and there, their social lives had not suffered.

"My children have a better social life than I do," Nicole said to Trish one day at lunch. Nicole and Trish went out to eat on Fridays, it was a treat for Nicole before becoming a mom taxi for the weekend.

"Well, the kids don't lie in bed all the time," Trish replied, looking away.

Nicole was stunned. "I don't lie in bed all the time," she responded.

Trish looked at Nicole. "What did you do last night?" she asked.

Nicole pushed her food around on plate, suddenly not hungry anymore. "I watched TV in bed," Nicole responded.

"There you go." Trish reached her hand across the table and squeezed Nicole's hand. "You have got to get out more. Have you tried any online dating sites?"

"No, I don't want to meet someone online. That just seems so creepy," Nicole replied.

"Okay, you leave me no choice but to set you up with one of Matt's single friends," Trish teased. "I think some of them might have potential."

Nicole grimaced. "Why don't we just let fate take its course? I will meet someone at some point."

"Well, you are going to have to get out of bed for fate to take its course, you hear me girlfriend?" Trish replied.

Nicole eventually agreed to a few blind dates, but she never could find a man she wanted to spend time with, let alone touch her. One night after her second date with Peter, she was unlocking her door when she felt his arms go around her waist and he murmured in her ear, "What about an invite for a little nightcap?" as he kissed her neck.

Nicole thought she was going to jump out of her skin. "No, Peter," Nicole replied, trying to untangle herself from his grasp. "I don't think that's a good idea, but thank you for dinner tonight."

Peter ran his hands through his perfectly coifed hair and sighed. "I was told you would take time to warm up to me, but I never expected you would be this cold. Goodnight, Nicole." He turned around and walked straight to his car, leaving Nicole standing in her doorway.

Nicole shut the door behind herself and sighed. 'I am not cold,' she said to herself. 'I am not cold. I just haven't found the right man. And I will be dammed if I let the first man I date, think he can feel me up.'

The kids had spent the weekend with Charles, so they weren't aware of her disastrous date the night before and didn't see the pint of ice cream in the trash she had eaten as she sat on the kitchen floor. The kids helped Nicole set the dinner table.

Gracie put the plates on the table and Ben put ice in the glasses and filled them with water. Nicole realized as they were eating that the children seemed very quiet.

"How was your weekend with your dad?" Nicole asked.

Ben and Gracie exchanged glances and replied in unison, "Good."

Nicole was immediately aware something was going on. She and her children had a very open relationship and dinner was always a boisterous time, with laughing and conversations about their day. This behavior was not normal.

"So, what did you do this weekend with your dad?" Nicole asked, trying a different approach.

Ben glanced at Gracie and put his fork down.

"Mom, I think you should know what's going on," Ben stated. "Dad and Whitney are getting married. She is pregnant."

Nicole's fork fell to her plate with a clatter.

"Mom." Gracie came around the table and hugged Nicole. "Are you okay?"

Nicole took a minute and replied, "Yes, sweetie." She reached across the table, grabbed Ben's hand and hugged Gracie back.

"Yes, I am okay, it's just a bit of a shock, you know?" Nicole replied.

Ben and Gracie let loose of all the news from the weekend, from Charles telling them about the wedding and baby, then Whitney telling them they were going to be the "best" step-brother and sister to the new baby. Nicole took it all in and, surprisingly, didn't feel as hurt as she thought she would.

Later, after the children were in their rooms and she had cleaned up the kitchen, she called Trish. She didn't mention what the children had told her and got straight to the point.

"Trish, you said a bunch of the girls were going out next Friday night, can I come too?" Nicole asked.

"Sure. It's about time you got out," Trish said.

"Can I have a beer?" Nicole asked the bartender.

"Nicole Berger?"

Part Two

Nicole was in the kitchen at Brad's house, fixing dinner. Brad and Nicole spent every spare moment together and feeding both sets of their children because it was easier to prepare a meal at Brad's home than in the small kitchen at the condo. Tonight, Nicole's mother was invited to dinner, and she sat at the breakfast bar, sipping a glass of chardonnay while watching Nicole put dinner dishes on the table.

"So, how it everything going?" mother asked.

Nicole smiled. "Mom, I couldn't be happier. This relationship is everything I never had before." Nicole hesitated and looked around the room. She refused to speak ill of Charles within earshot of the children, not that he followed the same rules when he had the children in his care.

"I feel good about this relationship. We share the same interests and I miss him terribly when he isn't around."

"Well, this is good news." Nicole's mom replied. "The princess has finally kissed her frog."

"Mom! Stop it. It's not like that at all." Nicole wiped her hands on a dishtowel and looked out the kitchen window at the kids playing in the pool. "It's like I finally got everything I wanted in life. A man whom I love, happy children and a great family. I finally found my match."

"And you think I drink too much wine! How much have you had?" Her mom picked up Nicole's wine glass to study the contents.

"Mom," Nicole stated, taking the wine glass away. "I don't need wine to make me feel the way I do about the way things are going with Brad and the kids. I have everything I ever wanted in this rag tag life we've pieced together. I have found my finally forever."

"I am so happy for you, my sweet girl." Nicole's mom cradled her face in her hands and kissed her forehead. "I want you to be happy, and Brad seems to make you happy. That's all a mother could hope for."

Out in the hallway, Brad leaned against the wall. He had been eavesdropping on the conversation between Nicole and her mother. He realized what he needed to do and decided not to waste any more time. He coughed to make his presence known, then rounded the corner and came into the kitchen.

He kissed Nicole and said, "Are you ready for me to light the fire for dinner?" and gently smacked her bottom.

Nicole giggled and replied, "Yes, please start the grill. I am ready for you to light my fire." She gave Brad a kiss.

Nicole's mom grabbed the chardonnay and refilled her glass. "You two need a cold shower." She went out to watch the children swim.

Later in the evening, Brad took Nicole's mother aside while Nicole and the kids cleaned up the kitchen.

"Claire," Brad started, "I wanted to talk to you about Nicole."

"Okay, Romeo. What do you want to talk about?" Claire asked. Brad sighed. Obviously, Claire would need a ride home tonight.

"I would like to ask your permission to ask Nicole to marry me. To become my wife," Brad said quietly.

Claire didn't say anything for a minute and then tears filled her eyes. "You promise you will take good care of my girl?" Claire asked. "You know I was so worried about her and the kids after that freaking Chuck destroyed her."

Claire went and stood right in front of Brad and grabbed his arms.

"Will you promise never to hurt her and take good care of her and my grandchildren?"

Brad took Claire's hands in his and said sincerely, "Claire, I promise I will never intentionally hurt Nicole, and I will protect her with all that I have."

Claire hesitated, then grabbed Brad in a big hug and answered, "Yes, you can marry my girl, Brad. I think she will be so happy with you."

Brad looked over Claire's shoulder and saw Nicole looking out the window at them both with a puzzled look on her face. He made a drinking motion with his hand and Nicole smirked and turned around.

Brad said, "Claire, let's say your goodbyes and I'll give you a ride home."

"You got it, Romeo." Claire went inside to kiss her grandchildren and Nicole goodnight.

Later, Nicole was dozing in Brad's arms when he asked, "Hey, babe, do we have the kids this weekend?"

Brad knew full well that they didn't have the children over the weekend, but it was part of his plan.

Nicole thought for a minute and replied, "No, both sets of kids are with the Ex's."

Brad grinned and asked, "Well, let's go on a date Saturday night. What do you think?"

Nicole snuggled in closer and answered, "I think that sounds wonderful."

Brad was working hard to make Saturday night a surprise for Nicole. He was so pleased with himself that on Friday night, Nicole made a comment over dinner.

"You have a mischievous look on your face. Are you up to something, Brad?" she asked.

"Who, me?" Brad tried to look shocked. "You know I don't have any secrets from you, babe. I was just thinking about you in that little pink number you bought a couple weeks ago and hoping you would wear it this weekend," he said with a wink.

Nicole blushed and grinned. "I think I can make that happen," she said and winked back.

Saturday night couldn't come quick enough for Brad. He had called his friends at the bar and they had reserved a table for Brad and Nicole. He also let Trish know about the plan and where he was going to ask Nicole to marry him so she wouldn't be surprised. Saturday night arrived, and Brad was beside himself. He knew with all his heart that asking Nicole to marry him was the absolute right decision. Brad opened the door to Wally's Bar and Grill and stood back to let Nicole go in and then entered behind her, only to come face to face with Lynette. His ex-wife.

"Well, I guess they let just anyone in this bar," Lynette stated, standing in front of Brad with her arms crossed over her chest.

"I thought you had the kids tonight?" Brad asked.

"Ever heard of a babysitter?" Lynette asked. Brad wanted to get away from her as soon as possible.

"Okay Lyn. Have a great evening," Brad responded. By then, Nicole had turned around and walked back to Brad and Lynette.

"Hi, Lynette," Nicole said and leaned in to give the other woman a hug. Brad sighed. He knew that Nicole and Lynette got along well, much better than he had ever gotten along with Lynette.

Lynette hugged Nicole back and said to Brad, "At least one of you is friendly tonight."

Nicole laughed and said, "Why don't you come sit down and have a drink with us?" as she looked back at Brad.

Brad thought he was going to faint. He didn't want his ex-wife sitting at the table with Nicole and him on the night he was going to propose.

"Oh, you are so sweet, Nicole, but I can't," Lynette replied. "I can't stay much longer. I must go home and relieve the babysitter, but that was nice of *you* to ask," Lynette glared at Brad.

Nicole patted Lynette's arm and said, "Okay, be safe. We will be over tomorrow to pick up the kids." Nicole turned back to Brad.

"Better treat this one better than you treated me, Brad," Lynette called out and then turned around and walked out of the bar.

Brad and Nicole took their seats at a table that had been reserved for them. If Nicole thought having an empty table available in the busy bar was out of the ordinary, she didn't mention it. Brad ordered a couple beers and put his arm over the back of Nicole's chair. The band was one of their favorites and they both enjoyed the music. Brad had arranged with Tim, who was in the band, to play one of Nicole's favorite songs, "Brown-Eyed Girl", and after they danced, he was going to get down on one knee and propose.

The evening was going perfectly, and after two beers, Brad was starting to relax. The lead singer of the band, Matthew, looked over at Brad and nodded his head. That was the signal that the band was going to play the song. At that very moment, Nicole stood up, leaned over and said in Brad's ear, "I'm going to the ladies' room. I'll be back in a minute." She turned to leave.

Brad about yelled out, "Wait," but didn't want to blow his surprise. He caught Matthew's eye and made a motion across his throat to stop the song. Matthew and the band quickly huddled and changed songs. Brad leaned back and sighed heavily. He hoped there wouldn't be any more surprises tonight, but he was wrong.

Nicole came back from the bathroom and called out, "Brad, look who I ran into, you remember Trish, right?" Trish smiled at Brad and sat down at the table. Brad feebly smiled back as the two ladies chatted away. He pulled out his phone and found Trish's name. Brad and Nicole had gone out to dinner with Trish and Matt a couple of times and Brad thought they were a good couple to know, but what was Trish doing here tonight?

Brad texted Trish. "You know tonight is the night I am going to ask Nicole to marry me. Feel free to stick around, but she doesn't know anything about it. Cool?"

Trish felt her phone vibrate and looked at the screen. A slow smile came over her face and she yelled, "Yes!" She texted back, 'That's why I was hiding in the back of the bar!'

So much for keeping it cool, Brad thought.

"What's going on?" Nicole asked. "Is everything all right?"

"Everything is perfect, girl. Mind if I stick around for one more song?" Trish asked.

Brad had only proposed once before in his life, to Lynette, and they had been a little tipsy, so he had said something like, "You want to get hitched?"

Tonight, Brad wanted everything about this proposal to be perfect, and everything was going wrong. Nicole had to use the bathroom, then she had to take a call from Ben about a form he needed signed for soccer in the morning. "Your father can sign it, sweetie," she had replied.

Finally, the band started playing the song that Brad had requested and he grabbed Nicole's hand

and said, "Let's dance!" Nicole glanced at Trish, who replied, "Go ahead. I am going to get another beer."

"*You're my brown-eyed girl...*" the lead singer sang. Brad's gaze was fixed on Nicole's face. Never had he felt so much love for a woman, and he couldn't imagine life without her. Nicole was laughing and singing along with the song, with no idea what was about to happen.

The song ended, and with a glance from the lead singer, Brad grabbed Nicole's hand and said, "Wait a minute, babe, there is something I want to ask you."

Nicole had a quizzical look on her face as Brad said, "Nicole, I love you very much." The bar was getting quiet. "And I want to ask you something." The bar was getting quieter. Brad held onto Nicole's hand and slowly got down on one knee. He pulled the ring box out of his pocket and opened it for her to see the two-carat princess cut engagement ring. "Nicole, love of my life, will you marry me?" Brad asked.

Nicole clamped her hand over her mouth as her eyes filled with tears. Brad looked around and asked again, "Nicole—marry me?"

With that second question, Nicole yanked her hand out of Brad's and turned and ran out the door, leaving Brad down on one knee in the middle of an empty dance floor in a bar where a person could hear a pin drop. Trish ran after Nicole and Matthew from the band jumped off the stage and pulled Brad to a standing position.

"Sorry, man," he said and then hopped back on stage and started a loud song.

Brad slowly walked to the exit that Nicole had run out of, to see Nicole crying in Trish's arms. As he approached the car, Trish looked up and gave Brad a sad smile.

Brad unlocked the car and said quietly to Nicole, "Get in the car, I will take you home."

The drive was quiet. Nicole had stopped crying but kept her head turned toward the window.

When Brad pulled into the driveway, Nicole opened the door quickly and jumped out of the car.

Brad put the car in park and raced up the stairs behind her.

"Babe!" Brad asked as he turned to Nicole to face him. "Can we talk about what just happened? Please?"

Nicole turned back, unlocked the door and said, "Come in."

Brad pulled the door shut behind them and followed her into the living room. He sat down next to Nicole on the sofa. "Do you want to tell me what's going on here?" Brad asked. Nicole sprang off the sofa and started pacing the floor.

"You proposed to me in a bar. *In a bar!*" Nicole yelled.

Brad was shocked. He replied, "But that's where we met."

"No, that's not where we met, Brad. We met in high school, or don't you remember that?" Nicole continued pacing back and forth. "We sat in that bar two years ago, talking about how we will never get married again, and then you pull a stunt like that tonight. I don't know what to believe. You told me you never wanted to get married again and then you asked me to marry you in the same bar?" Nicole asked.

"It wasn't a stunt," Brad softly replied.

"You don't propose to someone in a bar." Nicole threw her hands up in the air. "I think you wanted the attention of everyone watching you asking me to marry you."

"That's enough," Brad said as he stood up. "I wasn't making this about me; I thought I was making it about us spending the rest of our lives together."

"I think it's a good idea for us to take some time apart," Nicole said. She had stopped pacing and was looking down at her hands.

"What?" Brad asked. "I think you are taking this too far, Nic. I am sorry I proposed to you in a bar. I wasn't prepared for this kind of reaction. I thought you would be happy."

"I just need you to leave," Nicole replied.

"You are making a big deal out of this," Brad replied as he stood to leave. "You need to chill out." As soon as Brad said it, he wished he could take it back. "Get out!" was the response he received.

When he left, Nicole was so furious, she was shaking. "How dare he do something so juvenile?"

She grabbed her cell phone and called Trish.

When Trish picked up, Nicole asked, "Did you know about tonight, Trish?"

"Whoa, hold on there, Nicole" Trish answered. "I am your friend. Please don't jump on me like this."

"Sorry," Nicole replied. "I just had a huge fight with Brad, and he left." Nicole sat down on the sofa. "I don't know if I will ever see him again."

"Girl, now, you are being dramatic," Trish replied. "He will come around. And yes, I knew he was going to propose to you tonight a few days ago. Do I think it was romantic, sure? But obviously, you do not. Care to tell me why?"

Nicole took a deep breath and said, "I always pictured a proposal as private and romantic. He asked me to marry him in a bar, on a dance floor. I felt everyone's eyes on me, and I couldn't stand the feeling. Am I really crazy? I ran out on the man I love and, just a few minutes ago, ordered him out of my house."

Trish sighed. "I wish you would have told him that beforehand, but you didn't know he was going to propose tonight. You know Brad, he is such an extrovert, and you, my dear, are not. What happened tonight was in Brad's comfort zone, definitely not yours."

"But you would think he would know that, Trish," Nicole responded. "We have been together for over two years."

"Maybe its best you two do take a breather. It sounds like you are both pretty riled up about tonight," Trish replied.

"Thanks, Trish, I really appreciate you. Now go to bed and I'll call you tomorrow," Nicole said.

"Goodnight, Nicole. Try to get some rest," Trish replied and hung up.

Nicole looked at her hands and around the empty condo. For some reason, she knew she wasn't going to get much sleep tonight.

A week later, Brad got up to answer the door after he heard the doorbell ring. He opened it, to find Nicole standing on his front steps.

"You look awful!" Nicole exclaimed.

Brad grimaced. He looked down and took in his sweatpants and wrinkled t-shirt. "I didn't know there was a dress code for getting dumped by the woman you love," Brad replied.

Nicole looked down at her shoes. "Touche."

Both Brad and Nicole stood glancing at each other, neither knowing what to say next.

"Can I come in, Brad?" Nicole asked. Brad stepped aside and gestured for Nicole to come inside his house. She looked around the living room, noting the pizza boxes and empty beer cans. She sat down on the edge of a chair while Brad sat back down on the sofa.

"How have you been?" Nicole asked, looking intently at Brad.

"Living the dream," Brad replied. "Can't you tell?" He swept his hand over the cluttered coffee table.

"I am being serious, Brad," Nicole said. "I have wanted to call, but I didn't know what to say, or where to begin."

"Well, you could begin by telling me why my asking you to marry me was such a turn off to you?" he asked.

Nicole replied, "I can still see you are angry with me."

"I am not angry with you, Nic. I am hurt. I was so nervous about asking you to marry me, and after the response you gave me, I am not sure I know what to do with us anymore," Brad said.

Nicole looked down at her hands and nodded. "I understand."

The silence in the room was deafening.

"Brad," Nicole began. "I am sorry. I'm sorry for causing you any hurt feelings. I am sorry for the angry words I said to you. I have spent the last week trying to figure out my feelings and why I said what I did."

"So, did you figure it out?" Brad asked.

"Well, not really," Nicole responded. "The only thing I could think of was the proposal was just a shock to me."

Brad asked, "How so? We have been together for a long time. I thought we wanted to spend the rest of our lives together."

"Yes, that's true," Nicole said as she got up and moved to sit beside Brad on the sofa. "But we never talked about it. I think we should have discussed it before you proposed."

"Why should we have talked about it, Nic? So, you could worry about it? So, you could do a pro and con list about our relationship?" Brad responded.

"That's a little harsh, don't you think?" Nicole asked as she straightened up.

Brad rubbed his hand over his unshaven face and looked away from Nicole.

"Do you want me to leave, Brad?" she asked.

"No," Brad replied, looking directly at Nicole. "I want to figure it out, right here and right now, if you and I are going to make this work and if we want to stay together as a couple."

Nicole already had a plan in mind but she replied to Brad, "I'll see you Thursday at Wally's at 5."

Brad watches confused as Nicole leaves his house.

On Thursday, Nicole sat at the end of the bar, twisting a beer bottle back and forth between her hands and keeping an eye on the front entry. This was the first time she had been back at the bar since the night Brad had proposed to her. She was taking a risk in asking Brad to meet her for a drink. Brad walked into the bar, looked around, locked eyes with Nicole and broke into a big smile. Nicole smiled back. Brad came over and kissed her on the cheek.

"Hey, babe," he said as he sat down. The bartender pulled out a beer and placed it in front of Brad.

"Cheers!" Nicole said as she and Brad clinked the beer bottles together.

"So, what are we doing here, Nic?" Brad asked as he took a swing of beer.

"Well, after we talked last week, I thought we needed a fresh start. We both like coming here and

I didn't want to stop coming with you because, well, um, you know what happened last time we were here," she replied.

"Oh, I have been since then. Just not with you," Brad said. "But it wasn't much fun."

Nicole smiled. "I never thought I would be considered fun, so thank you for that."

"What?" Brad asked. "You are a lot of fun. I wouldn't be here if you weren't."

They spent the next hour talking and laughing, and it felt so good.

"Babe," Brad said. "I hate to be a wet blanket, but I have got to go. I have an early meeting in the morning."

"Okay," Nicole replied. She was slightly disappointed but knew neither one of them needed to be out late.

As they walked to her car, she looked up at the night sky. "Look at all the stars, what a beautiful night."

"I am looking at a beautiful sight," Brad responded as he stared directly at Nicole. They both held their gaze as he leaned in to kiss her. It was a gentle but passionate kiss which left Nicole breathless. As Brad drew her in for a hug, Nicole whispered, "Ask me again."

"What?" Brad asked, leaning back to look at Nicole.

"Ask me again," Nicole whispered, looking intently into Brad's eyes.

"Okay." Brad laughed. "Just to be sure. You know we are in a bar parking lot, right?"

"Yes," Nicole laughed.

"Here goes. Nicole, will you—" But Brad never got to finish his sentence.

"Yes, yes, yes!" Nicole said and leaned in for another kiss. "I want to marry you. I want to be your wife."

Two weeks later, "A white dress?" Nicole's mother asked. "That's a bold color choice for a second wedding."

"Mom. Stop." Nicole insisted. "You promised you would behave if you came dress shopping with me."

"All right. I will behave," Claire replied. "You will look beautiful in any dress you pick."

Nicole put on the next dress and stepped out of the dressing room with the help of the saleswoman. She stepped up on the dais and looked at herself in the mirror. Behind her, her mom brought her hand up to her mouth and tears formed in her eyes. Nicole looked back at her and slowly nodded.

Gracie said quietly, "Mom, you look like a princess."

Nicole smiled. "Well then, we have found the perfect dress. I always wanted to be a princess for a day," she said as she smoothed her hands over the dress.

Everyone in the room, including the saleswoman, had tears in their eyes. The saleswoman looked over at Claire and whispered, "I love my job."

Nicole and Brad didn't want to spend a lot of their money on the wedding, since they were looking to buy a house together, and the thought of shelling out a lot of money at a ceremony didn't sit well with either of them. Nicole's mom had bought Nicole's wedding dress, she said it was the least she could do after the catastrophe of a dress Nicole wore when she married Charles. She murmured to the clerk as she paid for new dress, "If that neckline was any higher on her first dress, that dress would have been a turtleneck."

They both decided that Brad would wear a suit, no tuxedo. Nicole wanted both her and Brad's children at the ceremony, so there would be no formal attendants, just their children in new suits and dresses. They found a beautiful old home that held weddings, and by a stroke of luck, the weekend that they wanted to get married was available, with a large deposit, of course. Nicole initially balked at the price, but Brad put her fears to rest.

"Nic, I can afford this, let me do this for us. Because," he said with a grin on his face as he pulled her close, "this is the last time I am getting married." Then he kissed her.

Nicole was elated; the venue was perfect. Trish was not upset about not being in the wedding, as she was finally expecting a baby. "No way am I walking down an aisle looking like a beached whale." But she was thrilled she was pregnant and smiled as she looked down and gently rubbed her baby bump. Not that she would be left out of the planning, Trish did offer to help with the simple decorations and finding a florist.

As the wedding date approached, Nicole had a full-blown panic attack. "What if this is a huge mistake?" she asked Trish at work. "I can't go through another divorce."

"I agree," Trish replied. "I barely got you out of bed after the breakup with Charles."

"What do I do?" asked Nicole.

Trish looked at Nicole. "Well, first, quit talking to me and go talk to the man you're in love with."

Nicole texted Brad. 'Are you free for lunch today?'

He quickly texted back. 'Can we eat at my office? I am too busy to go out right now.'

'Sure,' Nicole replied. 'I'll pick up some sandwiches and see you later.'

Nicole arrived at 12:30 and the office staff welcomed her as she went back to Brad's office. His assistant, Carol, whispered to Nicole, "I have never seen him happier." She knocked once and opened the door to his office. Brad smiled and stood up. Nicole's stomach was doing flip flops.

"Hey, babe," Brad said as he came around the desk to give her a kiss. "What did I do to get this surprise visit?"

Nicole dropped in the chair and said, "Brad, are we making a mistake?"

Brad sat on the edge of his desk and looked at Nicole. "I guess the question is, Nic, do you think we are making a mistake by getting married?"

Nicole's eyes filled with tears as she gazed out the window. "Nic," Brad said. "Where is this coming from? You and I are good, right?"

He stood up and sat down next to Nicole. "Look at me," Brad said.

Nicole turned her face to Brad and looked him in the eye.

"I love you, Nicole, with all my heart. I'll admit, I was the one who had doubts at first, but honestly, I can't think of anyone else I want in my life except you. When I asked you to marry me, it wasn't something that I just casually thought up. I want us to be together. Forever. I want to marry you, and I don't think that decision is a mistake. Do you understand me?"

Nicole looked at Brad and could see how serious he was about what he had said to her.

"I am so sorry, Brad. I don't know where this panic comes from. I love you more than anything and I am sorry I ever doubted you and us. Will you forgive me?" Nicole whispered.

Brad stood up and pulled Nicole up to him for a hug and a soft kiss. "Yes, I forgive you. Not a lot of gals can handle this sexy engaged man. I will leave that job up to you, and only you, okay, babe?"

"Yes," Nicole responded with a kiss.

"Now, babe, where is our lunch? I am starving," Brad asked as he stepped back and gazed at Nicole. He knew in his heart that she was the right fit for him. Of that, he had no doubt.

Nicole had everything ready for the wedding, her dress, the venue, the flowers, the reception meal, all thanks to Trish. Nicole and Brad were watching TV when Nicole asked, "What are you wearing to our wedding?"

"As little as possible," he replied, taking a drink of beer.

"No, I am serious," Nicole said. "I know you aren't a 'tuxedo' guy, but have you thought about what you are going to wear?"

"Hmm," Brad looked perplexed. "I guess I haven't really thought about it."

"Brad!" Nicole sat straight up on the sofa. "Our wedding is two weeks away!"

Brad looked at her. "What do you want me to wear?"

"Do you have a suit I don't know about?" Nicole asked as she stood up and started back toward Brad's bedroom.

"Whoa, hold on there a minute, Nic." Brad jumped up and quickly followed Nic to his bedroom. He reached the closed door at the same time Nicole did and held the handle to keep the door shut.

"Why are you acting so funny?" Nicole asked, "I have been in your bedroom before, in case you don't remember," with her eyebrows raised and a smirk on her face.

"I haven't picked up in the last couple days and I don't want you to see my mess," Brad replied.

The truth was he had purchased Nicole's wedding band and didn't want her to see it on the top of his dresser.

"Okay," Nicole said as she crossed her arms over her chest.

"You go in and get dressed and I will wait in the living room. You can model what you think you are wearing to our wedding." She turned and walked down the hallway. "I would start now if I were you, so I don't have to go in there and dress you myself."

Brad groaned. He knew Nicole was enjoying this situation too much.

So, when he rounded the corner in the living room in plaid shorts and a Hawaiian print shirt, Nicole couldn't help but laugh.

"No!" she said pointing her finger back to the bedroom. "Try again."

Of course, the second outfit was a green suit he had worn for St Patrick's day last year.

"No!" Nicole laughed. "The only green at my wedding is going to be on the flowers. Try again!"

"How about a wet suit?" Brad called over his shoulder as he walked back to his bedroom.

"Not a chance, Mister," Nicole teased. "But you can put it on for me after the wedding."

"Be careful what you ask for," Brad called out. "That wet suit will make you want me on the spot."

Nicole shook her head, wondering what crazy outfit he was going to come out in next. After a few minutes, Brad called out, "Are you ready for me?"

"Yes, love," Nicole answered. "What crazy outfit do you have on now?"

As Brad came around the corner, Nicole looked up and gasped.

"What?" Brad replied. "I thought you would like this."

She rose from the sofa and walked over to him. He had on a light gray suit and a white, button-down shirt underneath. He looked amazing.

"I have never seen you wear a suit before, Brad," Nicole whispered. "You look fantastic. I am stunned."

Brad chuckled and looked down at himself, pulling at the sleeves and the lapel of the coat.

"I wore this suit to my dad's funeral a couple years ago and forgot that I had it. Do you really like it?" he asked.

Nicole stepped back to survey him once more.

"I absolutely love it," she replied. "Are you sure you want to wear it again after your dad's funeral?" Nicole asked. Brad paused for a minute and then pulled Nicole close.

"Yes, I do. My dad would have loved you and I want to make new memories wearing this suit to marry you. Does that sound corny?"

"From you, yes, it does." Nicole laughed. "I would have loved to have met your dad. Thank you for being so thoughtful. I love you so much."

"I love you, too, Nic," Brad responded. "Because if you don't like this, I have a Santa suit I want to show you."

"We are so going through your closet," Nicole laughed. "After we get married."

It was the night of the wedding rehearsal dinner. The wedding was going to be an intimate affair, so the rehearsal for the ceremony didn't take long. Nicole had tears in her eyes as she walked down the aisle with Ben on one side and Gracie on the other. The last time she had walked down the aisle to be married, she was a child; now, she felt she really knew what love was.

Brad was a little misty-eyed too. Nicole's mom had a friend who knew a friend who was a minster, and he agreed to marry Nicole and Brad. They had met with him about a week ago to discuss the ceremony and the vows.

"Do you want to write your own vows or go the traditional route?" Reverend Gregory asked.

Nicole glanced at Brad and replied, "I am guessing traditional vows."

"Wait a minute," Brad said, turning to Nicole. "I think I want us to write our own vows."

Nicole looked shocked. "Brad, I want you to take this seriously."

"I am Nic. Look; we have both been married before. I hope that's not a shock to you, Reverend." Brad glanced at Reverend Gregory and winked. "So, hear me out. I want to say to you what I want you to hear, not something everyone has repeated. I won't take long or make any jokes if that's what you're worried about. This is out of my comfort zone, you know that, but I want to do that for us. What do you think?"

Nicole touched Brad's face and whispered, "I love you so much."

She turned to Reverend Gregory and said, "I guess we are writing our own vows."

The day of the wedding arrived. Nicole and her mom were at the wedding venue putting the last-minute touches on Nicole's hair and makeup.

Claire took Nicole's hands and said softly, "You are a beautiful bride, darling. You will take his breath away."

Nicole smiled and hugged her mom. "Thank you for all you did to help me get here, Mom. I love you."

The door to the bridal room opened and Trish walked in. "Wow, look at you! You look amazing."

Trish said to Nicole's mom, "It's time to take your seat, let's get this girl married."

Ben and Gracie came into the room and hugged their mother.

"Are you ready, guys?" Nicole asked.

Both children answered, "Yes," simultaneously.

"Let's go," Nicole responded, linking her arms into her children's, "Time to get your mom married!"

Brad couldn't take his eyes off the vision that was walking down the aisle. As the trio approached the altar area, Brad came down the stairs, hugged Gracie and whispered, "You look so pretty, Gracie." Then he reached over to shake Ben's hand. "My mom has been through a lot," Ben said quietly. "I want your promise that you will take good care of her for us."

"You have my word," Brad replied.

With that consent, Ben took his mother's hand and placed it in Brad's. Together, they walked up the steps and stopped in front of Reverend Gregory. Both Brad and Nicole stared into each other's eyes, unable to look away.

The minister began the service and said the usual quotes about marriage, but Brad and Nicole were oblivious. Revered Gregory had to clear his throat to get their attention.

"Nicole, you may begin with your vows." Nicole glanced down at the note she had wadded up in her hand, but she knew the words by heart.

"Brad, my love. You saved my life. I was in a deep place that I didn't know how to get out of, and you pulled me back to the surface. You have shown me how to laugh and how to love again. You never gave up on us, even when I had doubts. You are my forever love, my final, forever love. I love you with all my heart and I put my trust in you for our future together as a family," Nicole said as she finished her vows.

Brad had to take a minute, and he doubted for a split second if he could even respond. What Nicole had said was one of the most beautiful tributes anyone had said to him in his entire life.

He finally took a deep breath and began his own vows. "Nicole, I have known you since high school, but until I met you again, I realized I didn't know what a special person you are, but I do now. The way you love everyone, including me, with all your being, I have never seen anything like it. You are a ray of sunshine in my life that I never had before, and I don't ever want anything to block that sunshine. Even today, the words you just said to me are the kindest words that anyone has ever spoken to me. I will protect you and the kids with my life for as long as I live, and I will cherish you for the gift that you are to me. I love you, Nic," Brad replied as he brushed a tear off Nicole's cheek.

Both Nicole and Brad could hear sniffles in the audience, but they only had eyes for each other. Reverend Gregory led them through the ring ceremony and then prayed over them.

"Lord, bless this couple as they navigate their lives together. Help them celebrate their victories and hold them together through the tough times. But most importantly, let the love we have seen here today between them be a constant love they can cherish for the rest of their lives. Amen."

Brad smiled at Nicole and winked. "Now, here comes the good part!" he whispered.

The minister closed his Bible and announced to the crowd, "I am honored to present to you Mr. and Mrs. Brad Reynolds."

With that statement, Brad took Nicole in his arms and placed a long, gentle kiss on her lips. Both turned, hand in hand, and smiled to the crowd as they walked down the aisle.

The reception decorations were beautiful, and the room smelled of the fresh flowers that were on each table and scattered across the room. The head table, where Brad and Nicole were going to sit, had their children sitting on either side of them, since this was as a celebration for them as much as it was for Brad and Nicole. Light refreshments were being passed by waiters, and soft music was playing in the background.

Brad and Nicole entered the reception to the announcement of Brad's friend Kevin saying, "Here they are, let's welcome Mr. and Mrs. Reynolds."

There was loud applause as the bride and groom entered the room, full of their family and friends. Nicole looked around the room and was in awe of the decorations and the number of friends and family that were in attendance to celebrate their wedding. Trish and her husband came up to greet them.

Trish said, "That was the best wedding ceremony I have ever seen. And your vows, oh my goodness, there was not a dry eye in the house. Even he teared up," she said, pointing at her husband.

"What can I say?" Matt replied, "You both deserve this life to live together. I am a softie when it comes to love."

As Nicole and Brad made their way around the room, greeting family and friends, Brad never let go of Nicole's hand for long, and occasionally, they would both stop to look at each other with a look of love and adoration.

"We really did it, Nic," Brad whispered at one point.

"Yes, we did," Nicole responded. "I don't think I have ever been this happy."

After they sat down and had a light snack, Nicole's mom came up behind them and suggested, "Why don't we have you two cut your cake?"

Nicole and Brad made their way to the cake area. The cake was decorated with edible flowers that gave the creation a magical appearance. Brad picked up the knife, and with Nicole's hand over his, they both cut a slice of cake and put the piece on a plate. Brad then cut the pieces of cake again, into smaller bites. The audience was cheering when Nicole and Brad each picked up a piece of the cake. Nicole reached up to put a slice in Brad's mouth, when, all of the sudden, Brad smashed his piece over Nicole's mouth. There was a collective gasp in the room and Brad took a quick glance to see everyone looking at them, some with their mouths hanging open. He turned to look back at Nicole to see her startled expression.

'*Oh, no,*' Brad thought, '*What have I done?*'

Suddenly, Nicole grabbed Brad's face and began kissing him, all the while smearing the cake and frosting all over his mouth and beard. The wedding crowd went wild, laughing and cheering. Brad and Nicole turned to the crowd, grinning, and kissed again. The photographer caught the moment.

It's the main picture hanging in their hallway today. Brad and Nicole laughing, their mouths and chins covered in cake and frosting. It was the beginning of their journey and their final forever.

On a busy morning, while trying to get the kids to school on time, Nicole paused in front of the picture, like she does frequently, smiled at the memory and lightly touched Brad's face in the picture. A pair of arms encircled her from behind and Brad kissed her neck.

He whispered, "Any regrets, my love?"

Nicole turned and said, "Yes. I have one regret. That I hadn't met you sooner!" And with a quick peck on his lips, Nicole began herding the kids out the door. But she did look behind her and saw that Brad was looking at the picture. And he was smiling too.

The End

About the Author

Ann Spencer is a nurse by day and spends her spare time reading and writing books. It was always a childhood dream for Ann to write and now the dream has come true with her first published work, "Finally, My Forever." Ann lives outside of Louisville Kentucky with her husband, a dog, cat & bird.

To connect with Ann Spencer, email her at: spencerannp@gmail.com.   or find her on social media:

www.facebook.com/ann.p.spencer

www.instagram.com/Loislane774

www.ingramcontent.com/pod-product-compliance
Lightning Source LLC
Chambersburg PA
CBHW070511030726
47503CB00004B/1234